REBOOTS

DIABOLICAL STREAK

REBOOTS
DIABOLICAL STREAK

MERCEDES LACKEY
CODY MARTIN

an imprint of

ARC
MANOR
Rockville, Maryland

ISBN: 978-1-61242-138-4

www.PhoenixPick.com
Great Science Fiction & Fantasy

Published by Phoenix Pick
an imprint of Arc Manor
P. O. Box 10339
Rockville, MD 20849-0339
www.ArcManor.com

PUBLISHER'S NOTE

THE ORIGINAL *REBOOTS* WAS PUBLISHED as part of our Stellar Guild series, which pairs a veteran author with a newer author of the veteran's choosing. Each of the writers constructs a story set in the same universe, complementing each other.

Mercedes Lackey chose a promising young writer, Cody Martin and together they created the universe of *Reboots*: a universe where paranormal creatures live side by side with regular humans...and who best then to take on the rigors of space flight.

Spaceships full of zombies, werewolves and vampires ... what could be better?

Not much, it seems like, and we decided it was a world that needed more material. It helped that we kept getting requests for a sequel.

Hence, *Reboots: Diabolical Streak*.

Other veteran authors who have participated in the *Stellar Guild* program include Larry Niven, Robert Silverberg, Kevin J. Anderson, Eric Flint, Harry Turtledove and Nancy Kress. For more information please visit **www.StellarGuild. com.**

DIABOLICAL STREAK

THE UNIVERSE HAD CHANGED IN some ways, but had stayed the same in many more. At least it seemed that way to the Boggart. He'd been around and actually active longer than most, save for some of the more adaptable Paras, nineteen centuries, give or take a decade. The modern age didn't particularly agree with many creatures of his ilk, what with its abundance of cold iron, lack of superstition from the Norms, and high technology that helped to illuminate the night that all of the dark and scrabbling beings used to inhabit. But then, Boggarts were more closely associated with humans, or "mortals" as the Fey and the Sidhe used to call them, than some of the other creatures that had come tumbling out of the broom closet at the start of the Zombie War.

Ah yes, the Zombie War; humanity first truly found out about the Paranormal when Zombies showed up. No one knew the how or why of Zombies, only that they didn't go after Paras. Paras—short for "Paranormals," the catchall for our kind—largely depended on humanity. Most of us for sustenance of one form or another; blood, psychic energy, offerings, whatever. The Zombie War and its outcome changed everything, the entire world turned upside down as Paras were integrated. We were integrated because we turned the tide of the war; humanity was losing against the onslaught of the dead. Paras were what tipped things back in favor of mankind, though the goodwill from the Zombie War didn't last long. Misunderstandings, massacres, more conflicts fought. Once humanity knew that Paras existed, well, humanity was creative and very good at destruction, and the Paras were losing the new war, even though it cost the Norms—catch-all term for anyone not "Para"—dearly. Then came the advent of deep space travel and that was the answer to everyone's problems; population pressure decreased by using Para crews, and the Paras could do what humans could not—live for decades, even hundreds of years on the sub-lightspeed ships. Zombies were rebranded as the politically correct Reboots, and put into useful roles where they weren't a danger to Norms. One politico had anguished at the time, "What in God's name can you do with twenty billion Zombies?" It turned out, if you were a corporation, creative, with no scruples, and had a lot of jobs too simple even for a bot, you could do a helluva lot.

It wasn't all wine and roses. There was a deep rot within the system. Corruption at the highest levels of government and corporate structures, and the fusion of both into the Home Service. Still, it worked while it was needed.

But nothing lasts forever, not even a truce. Now there was FTL, and some of the old tensions between Norms and Paras were boiling up again. It was an interesting universe, especially for a Boggart tryin' to make a few bucks.

Or, as the old French saying went, *plus ca change, plus c'est la meme chose.* He'd been hunted or exploited in one way or another for much of his long life, and at least in the modern age, he was his own boss. After the last gig he had done for remnant Home Service, he had been able to set up his own firm and bigger office, quickly followed by wiping his hands of anything attached to ol' HS. Part of that was that it was too much hassle working their jobs and running their errands, anymore. With FTL becoming widespread and affordable, Home Service seemed to think that a PI like Humph could trot from one end of the known 'verse to the other on a whim. That, and Home Service had lost the importance that they had once held. No longer were they in charge of exploratory expeditions and charting unknown systems for settlement, keeping a tight leash on their Para crews. Everything was outsourced to private companies now, with mixed human and Para crews that were much less dysfunctional. Well, except for the Fangs. The Fangs put the "fun" in "dysfunctional"….Increasingly, Fangs were happy snugged down in their nest-Stations and really didn't want "the adventure of space travel," which just meant more jobs for the other Paras. The profit margins were better and the liabilities were lower for everyone involved. In some systems, there was still a "boom town" sort of feeling, with lots of new wealth ready for the taking.

Not that everyone was pleased that Paras were becoming wealthier and more mobile. Political advocacy groups calling for stricter sanctions on specific types of Paras coupled with an increase in high-profile news stories featuring Paras as the villains…

After the job for HS, he had sat down and had a pow-wow with Fred and Skinny Jim. Earth was too hot for their little gang, and there wasn't nearly enough action there besides the never-ending job of chasing down deadbeat dads and cheating spouses. They had to find a place to set up shop; somewhere that they wouldn't stand out too much, but where they would still be able to sell their services for a decent price. Humph had a reputation for keeping his word and getting the job done, which meant something—namely credits—in a universe where a lot of beings would sell their own grandmother for the time of day. With that commodity, they shopped around. Stations were out, since there was always too much Were and Fang activity on those; the dens and nests would always want a slice of the pie, so to speak. Resort or garden worlds never had all that much going on for them; sometimes jobs would land there, but hardly did they ever start there. After mulling over the problem over a few bottles of whisky and a few pickled brain fungi for Jim, they finally found their new home: Planet Mildred.

Planet Mildred was perfect for Boggart, Barkes and Bot. It was a mid-sized industrial world, with grav that was Earth-Norm and no moon besides one that was tidally locked and never went full. Fred still had to stay indoors on "bad nights," but otherwise was relatively comfortable. As an industrial world, it had more than its fair share of spaceports and orbiting refueling platforms; combined with its location as a waypoint between anywhere someone would want to come from and anywhere someone would want to go, it made the quintessential travel hub. Everyone came through Mildred on their way to something else. It was never called Mildred, of course. The story Humph heard was that some drunken transport captain had named the planet after his waitress girlfriend. Most people just called it the Hub.

Basically, in terms of the old Noir Films, this was the Waterfront, the Warehouse/Industrial complex, Skid Row, and the Tenderloin districts from those old movies all combined. Maybe some Chinatown thrown in. And the whole planet was like that. Perfect for the three of them, they didn't stand out overly much, and there were always new marks with new tidbits of information, new crimes that the victims didn't want the cops to know about, new crimes that the cops couldn't or wouldn't solve, new gossip, and new job opportunities. Lots and lots of smuggling, which always opened up a job or three on a regular basis. And what they got was "petty" by crime standards. That was always good for keeping the money coming in while also keeping their profile low.

Humph had quite the cozy little setup; he had tossed his old place—the only thing he had kept was the ancient wooden desk—and bought a "business suite" near enough to one of the major spaceports that things were just comfortably shabby without being run down enough to scare off customers. Office in front, living quarters behind it—not that he needed much in the way of living quarters. Fred the Werewolf needed a room with no windows and a good, solid metal door, period. The few nights out of the year that there was enough moonlight to cause Fred to go all hairy and wild-eyed, he was able to lock himself down in the room without worrying about the door getting busted down. Skinny Jim the Zombie needed a corner; they'd found an old robot, gutted it so there was nothing but a shell and a couple bits to make him look authentic, and installed him inside with a disinfectant system to keep him from rot, and another to keep his skin properly oiled and pliant. When he wasn't at the computer…scratch that, he was always at the computer. And Humph himself needed somewhere to keep some clothes, a shower, and a bed. He'd initially thought having partners would drive him insane, and sometimes the other two did force him to retreat to the Other Space connected to his pocketwatch, but for the most part, they were almost eerily an ideal fit. Maybe it was Fred and Jim. They had spent the better part of a century and a half learning how to tolerate a hell of a lot, cooped up in an exploration ship with some of the biggest douchebag Fangs in the known 'verse, (which was saying something) and by contrast, the firm was Mellowville. And neither of the boys were exactly going to set the world on fire with their looks. Despite the reputation for charisma that oozed from the very pores of Weres, that only applied to Alpha Weres, and Fred wasn't even a Beta, he was a Lone. He looked exactly like what he'd been before he got chomped; a balding, middle-aged engineer, though he had lost a few pounds and bulked up in the muscle department when you compared him to his Home Service mugshots. As for Jim, well, in disguise he looked like a second-hand bot. And out of disguise he was a Zombie, and an aged one at that.

Or maybe it was a match made in…wherever such matches were made. Probably someplace where virgin sacrifices were still a tolerated cost of doing business.

On the whole, things were comfortable for the trio. Their expenses were relatively low, and the jobs were steady, or at least they had been until a bit less than two months ago. The planet they were on was like that sometimes; usually an even flow of cheating spouses, embezzling partners, runaway teenagers, something being smuggled gone missing, someone needing something "taken care of" off the books, custody cases, and the odd bounty gig…the usual thing for a PI, even in the modern age. Humans—and most Paras, for that matter—never changed. Despite that, there had been slim pickings for longer than usual. The office wasn't hurting just yet, but the expense account wasn't as flush as it used to be; regular shipments of scotch, cigars, premium steaks, ammo, and rehydrated brains had been slowly eating away at their funds.

"*Woman Claims Gremlin Is Stalker,*" Humph read aloud from the news twits. "*Wrongful Death Ruled in Fur Silver-Poisoning Case. Self-Defense Verdict Sends Dwarf To Slammer.*" He shook his head. "Not a damn thing for us in the twit feed today, and am I just getting paranoid, or are there more stories out there lately about us being the Big Bad Boogiemen?"

Fred and Jim were seemingly lost in their own conversation; something deep and thought-provoking, no doubt.

"…I don't really care what studies you bring up, blondes are where it's at."

"You've got less brains than I do, Fido. Redheads, hands down, any day of the week. If you can come up with one good argument, I'll eat my own hand. No, really!"

The Boggart sighed. Not that either of the boys were going to get within ten nautical miles of a woman. Not by any stretch of the imagination were either of them the answer to a maiden's prayers. Or even a not-so-much-a-maiden. Fred even had trouble getting dates among his own kind. Being crammed in a small ship as the jack-of-all-work with a bunch of Fangs whose idea of a come-on was to just use the Vampiric hypno-power on a gal had not given him any instruction on the fine points of Picking Up Women. Humph had been trying to school him, but Fred was a slow learner on that subject, and pathetically oblivious to body language from the fairer sex. It didn't help that he had been a lone wolf for so many decades; apparently female Weres picked up on that, through pheromones or some supernatural ability.

The Boggart relit the stogie that he had going, leaning back in his chair. *Things have gotta pick up soon. I need something to get me out of the office, and to keep these two busy.* Not to mention keep all of them in brains, steak, and booze.

Secretly he'd always wanted to have the sort of shabby-film-noir detective office that was right out of one of his favorite PI movies. Preferably including the wise-cracking, gum-chewing secretary with a great pair of legs. Well, you couldn't have everything. He had the office now…just the secretary wasn't what you'd see in a movie. Instead of a leggy bleached blonde, Jim served in that capacity, usually sitting in the outer office when he wasn't playing cards with Fred. Humph had the bigger desk of the two in the second room, facing the door. Fred's desk was behind him, facing into the wall, as befitted the "junior partner." Since this was a securitized building, you had to phone when you hit the vestibule of the building to get in, which generally gave Jim plenty of time to get back into place.

"Wish that damn phone would ring," Humph grumbled aloud.

As if it had heard him, it did ring.

"Goddamnit boss, why didn't you wish for a lottery win instead? Or a baker's dozen of sexy, sex-starved blondes…" Fred mumbled, as Jim answered the phone. The light on the unit indicated that it was a call from the front door.

"Boggart, Barkes and Bot, how can I direct your call?" Jim was saying, as he trotted to his place, feet only clanking a little on the bare floor. "Yes, Mister Boggart is in, but he's on the phone with a client. He should be finished by the time you get up to our office; I'll buzz you on through."

"Mister? Been awhile since anyone tried throwing that one at me," Humph said to no one in particular. Glancing around his desk, he saw exactly how cluttered and messy it was, and clumsily began sweeping things off the top of it into drawers and under the chair. Fred watched Humph's efforts, shrugged, and kicked his feet up onto his own desk. Humph sighed. "Classy, jackass."

"It makes you look better, boss. Professional." Fred paused thoughtfully for a second. "Or what professional would look like if it were a few hundred years old and pickled in whisky." Well that was more what he wanted from Fred. Once a Lone Wolf didn't always mean a Lone Wolf; with the right circumstances, Fred could change his position in life, much as he had already done with his former crew-mates. Furs preferred to deal with their own kind when things got complicated enough to need the services of a firm like BBB. Having Fred play Chief Detective when a Fur case came up could cinch them the job that might have otherwise slipped through their fingers. Now, if only he'd learn all that a little faster...

"You're a laugh riot, mother—"

The door swung open then, cutting the Boggart off. He had just enough time to snatch up a file folder and open it, posing as if he were casually studying it instead of cleaning off his desk and cussing out his partner moments before.

"Mister Boggart is waiting for you, sir," Jim said brightly. "Go on in."

Somewhere in the back of his mind, the Boggart had pictured the client to be what they always were in the old vids...a curvy blonde with legs up to *there,* red, red lips and a voice that sounded as if she was always a little out of breath. At least that's what he always hoped for in clients, even if it was exceedingly rarely the case. It certainly wasn't in this instance.

Well, he'd gotten the blonde part right, but that was about all. Thin, mousey-blonde, with a face that looked as if he was simultaneously eating lemons and thinking about the pineapple someone had recently shoved up his ass. A conservatively cut gray business outfit. This dude wasn't money himself, but Humph's seventh sense told him that he represented money.

"Good afternoon, *gentlemen*." The suit said that word in such a way that it sounded like it pained him to associate it with Humph and Fred, even if only to keep custom. "My name is Bevins. You may refer to me as Mister Bevins. I represent Ms. Catherine Somerfield, who has requested me to acquire your services." Humph stood up for a moment, gesturing with one hand for Bevins to take a seat. He did not sit down.

Humph put the file he was holding down, casually flipping it so that it was right side up. "Is there a reason why Ms. Somerfield couldn't attend to this herself? Why send you, Mr. Bevins?" Something told Humph that there was big money attached to this case, if it was going to turn into a job he would take. Then again, they could really use any job at the moment. The boys wouldn't be too pleased if he got picky at this stage.

Bevins gave Humph the hairy eyeball. "I cannot say, Mr. Boggart. My employer is not accustomed to divulging her reasons for her actions to her employees, nor are her employees encouraged to speculate on her motives. I'm sure you understand."

"I do, but you have to understand our position as well, Mr. Bevins. We're not your boss's employees, yet. And while a go-between such as yourself might not be privy to her motives"—Bevins noticeably bristled at being called a go-between—"it does come as a factor for us." He took a puff on his cigar, regarding the suit. "That said, your boss can rely on our discretion in whatever matter she needs attended to; I imagine that's why she's using you in the first place. Discretion." Humph loved to make guys like this squirm. Just because they were in service to people with power and influence didn't mean that they were any better than the rest of the world; Humph took opportunities like this one to subtly remind people like Mr. Bevins of that fact.

Fred was watching the entire exchange with a bemused expression, keeping his feet up on his desk. *Watch and learn, boyo,* the Boggart thought. It wouldn't hurt to have two of them able to trade off as "boss," especially if Fred learned some better people skills, particularly among his own kind.

"What we need to know here, is fairly simple," the Boggart continued as Bevins' lips tightened. "Is this job going to involve anything skirting legalities?" He held up a hand before Bevins could answer. "Not to say that if it does, we won't take it. It just means that things get a lot more expensive—and if I find out *after* the fact that it does, you really do not want to consider what the fee will be, unless you can get your hands on something equivalent to the expense account of Home Service back when they still had a few red cents to rub together."

"The job, Mr. Boggart, is simple. I need you to find a man and bring him to me, relatively unharmed. This is aboveboard, but my employer wishes to keep this quiet. Family is involved, you see, and the company cannot be the center of a scandal anytime soon." He sneered, looking from Fred to Boggart. "I'm insulted that you would insinuate that my employer would ever be involved in procuring the services of anyone for less than sterling purposes. I've come to you, not for your apparently flexible morals, but because of your reputation of a being that always gets the job done. And that you can keep quiet about it afterwards." His expression softened marginally, as he appraised the Boggart. "Or have I heard incorrectly?"

Humph spread his hands, grinning wide enough to show his sharp teeth. "No, you've heard right, Bevins. Let's get down to particulars."

"The Case of the Missing Heir!" Skinny Jim rubbed his hands together. "With *our* skills, this should be a—"

"Hold it right there, don't jinx it," the Boggart warned, interrupting him. "We can gloat when it's over and the money's in the account. For now, assume everything that can go wrong, will." *A pessimist is never unpleasantly surprised,* he reminded himself.

"You are just a ray of sunshine, boss," Jim groused. "All right, Fred, I'll do the usual, you check on the company. Last one done buys the next meal." Which in Jim's case... could be expensive. Jim *could* eat the brain fungus he and Fred had found on the planet they'd taken refuge on. It grew just fine in the spare closet, and it would do in a pinch. He preferred the dehydrated animal brains you could get at the Zombie supply shop. But what he *wanted* was fresh. That got expensive. Even more expensive than Fred's preferred steaks—unless Fred was really treating himself to the beer-fed Kobe-style beef that could only be gotten imported from off-planet.

"Sounds like you two have your end of things well in hand. I'm going to head out, start hitting the pavement. Message me when you have a heading."

From everything Bevins had told him, the Boggart wasn't at all confident that old-fashioned shoe leather applied to cement was going to get him anywhere. But what he *was* sure of was that he needed to walk in silence for a while. He needed to mull over the interview that had just taken place, and let his instincts see what intel they could extract from it. Because something seemed...off.

Like his namesake, the Boggart did his best thinking when he was shuffling down an empty city street, making his way from pool-of-lamplight to pool-of-lamplight.

On the surface, this looked like a legit job, nothing that Humph would turn his nose up at even when business was good. The blue bloods regularly had guys like him do their dirty work so as not to sully their white-gloved hands. It was how the universe had worked for time beyond time, and that was just fine with him. If nothing else, it meant that there would always be a job for him. Still, he couldn't place his finger on what it was about this one that bothered him. Bevins was the usual snob that lackeys could be; he saw himself as climbing the ladder to someday reach the lofty heights where his employers sat, never mind how much of a delusion that probably was. The job wasn't unusual, a rich nobody had run off to the embarrassment of some rich somebodies, and needed to be fetched back. Par for the course.

Maybe that's it, he thought. *It's too simple, too normal. Whenever anything looks like it's going according to plan, it's probably not somehow.* Humph tried to shrug the feeling off, but he just couldn't shake it.

Well, all right then. Plan for the worst, hope for the best. Make sure he still had some favors owed, bolt-holes open, options in place. He pulled a microdot out of a hidden compartment in his watch, stuck it in his PDA, and opened the files. Just to be sure.

He frowned a little. There were fewer options open than he liked; still had some but…he made a note that if this panned out, it was time to spread the love around and buy himself a few more shady operators. It never hurt to have a few more cards to play when the chips were down. A little bail money here, a little bribe money there, and it all added up to favors owed. Favors that one day might mean the difference between nailing a case or ending up in a shallow grave.

Humph's comm unit chirped. He tapped a button, cueing up the earpiece he was wearing. "Boggart here, go ahead."

"It's me, boss. Got a lead for you." Fred was silent for a moment, and there was the sound of shuffling papers and data pads. "Looks like you're headed for the pleasure district on the east side, not too far from where you are now. That's the last place Jim found a cash withdrawal. Big one too. Looks like he was planning to find the original good time that was had by all."

"Wonderful. I'm heading there now. I'll be sure to say hi to your Ma, Fred."

"Don't bother," Fred quipped back. "She's too busy collecting all those nickels."

Humph had spent the next day and a half slogging all through the pleasure district before he finally hit paydirt. Humph didn't like going through there, even though his work forced him to tramp through often enough. Too many holo advertisements, bright even in full daylight. Too many shills too eager to entice him into their dens of "delight." As much of a city creature as he had become, it was also too crowded. Oxygen stations, brothels and sex clubs, trendy and exclusive bars with lines that stretched around the block, street vendors hawking everything from technological toys to sausages of dubious origin to the mostly legal drugs. All of it was pressed in on itself, commerce and vice squeezing into every crack and crevice that it could. He didn't much care for the crowds either. Too many Norms trying to look like Paras. Too many Paras pretending to like the Norms. Kids too young to be here, decked out in Fur tribal gear. Jaded adults trying to find something new to jazz themselves, wearing outfits he couldn't afford in a year's worth of jobs. Paras passing as the latter—but he knew them with a single sniff. A very few Paras not even *trying* to pass, but serving as the exotic shills at the doors of clubs and bars. Furs mostly, a few Satyrs, some things he didn't recognize at first glance. There were a lot of mythologies out there, and it seemed Old Earth was disgorging a little something new out of them all the time, as Norms got the trick of Invocations and Bindings. Not everyone was out of the broom closet voluntarily; some, like Humph, had been dragged out, kicking and screaming, by a Norm who had learned some magic and wanted a Para pet—or slave. You never saw Reboots, of course. They were tidied away behind the scenes where no one would have to look at them. It wasn't as if they had the capacity to *care*. Intelligent Reboots like Skinny Jim were one in a billion.

It was mostly Norms though; Mildred was hardly an exotic world. There wasn't much here to attract a Para that didn't have to be here. And as a hub for Norm trade, if there were any aliens on-planet, he'd never spotted them.

It had taken a little bit of effort, but not too much; the usual haunts were scoped out, palms of bouncers and madams were liberally greased, bartenders and maitre d's at some of the more upscale hotels and casinos were discreetly questioned, with credit chips passed along just as discreetly. He'd come across just what he was looking for when he bribed a senior bellhop into allowing him into a room that Harry frequently reserved when he *wasn't* on the lam; it turned out that he had been there just the night before, and the room hadn't been turned over yet. Humph found a crumpled receipt printed out from the desk net-unit. It was a confirmation for a reservation at a different hotel, not nearly as upscale but still way out of Humph's price-range, across town. Harry had made it under an assumed name, and it looked like he was paying with a quick-use cred card; it was the sort you could pick up for a preset amount. When bought with cash, they were nearly untraceable; no name was attached to them, and once they were empty you just threw them away and bought another one.

Untraceable, unless, of course, you could winkle out the card number from the receipt and the transaction. Well, he'd leave that to Skinny Jim and Fred if he somehow missed the mark at the new digs. He gave them a quick heads-up, and a scan of the receipt, and he was off. Rule number one of being a PI: Don't be stupid. Rule number two: If you have partners, *tell them where you're going*. Humph didn't much care for having the starring role in a chump comedy. If he got in a bind that he couldn't handle on his own, having his partners know where he was going would at least give them a heading for where to send the cavalry. Or the coroner, depending.

His destination was The Troposphere Hotel. It was done up to look old-fashioned, somewhere around the early to mid

20th century, while still having all of the modern amenities that the rich and shameless could want or need. Harry probably thought that it was a low-key place to lay low at, since it was a couple of rungs down the ladder from his usual accommodations, never mind the fact that it would have taken six months' worth of pay for someone like Humph to even spend a night there. *Monied myopia, sometimes the rich really like to make things easy for me.* Barging in through the front door wasn't going to be that much of an option, not this time; despite the evidence to the contrary, Harry might have been canny enough to bribe someone at the front desk to alert him if anyone suspicious came around. This called for something a lot more subtle, something that would get him quietly and seamlessly past the hotel security—which at this level of things, would have living bodies attached to guns along with the usual electronic surveillance.

First place to look, the service entrances. If there was any way of getting inside without attracting notice, it would be there. At the third one—at a guess, it looked as if it was somewhere around the restaurant area—Humph hit paydirt. There was a crew of workmen in paint-spattered coveralls loitering there, obviously on break. And from the look of them, this was a bunch hired from a temp-labor outfit; it seemed that none of them knew each other all that well. *Easy money.* Humph was wearing a general laborer outfit already for just such an occasion. It was the top of the hour, which meant their break was probably almost up; he confirmed it when they all started to put out their non-carcinogenic cigarette butts and get up. Humph was already in similar basic work clothes, old and worn enough that a lack of paint wouldn't be noticed. Invoking some fast and dirty magic quickly and putting on one of his generic faces with his glamour, Humph surreptitiously slipped into the group as they shuffled back inside.

He dropped to the back of the group as soon as they were inside, and kept his nose alert. The smell of hot water and strong bleach told him when they were near the laundry, and he slipped away, following the scent. It was easy enough to find a janitor's coverall—no Reboot janitors for this joint—and sneak it out of the pile waiting for pickup and distribution to the locker room.

Places like this didn't bother with ID tags, which could be duplicated, passed off to a friend, lost, or stolen. For low-level help like housekeeping and janitorial staff, they relied on RFID—radio frequency identification—tags sewn into the uniforms, uniforms which you had to put on when you arrived and take off when you left. Perfect for his purposes. A janitor tag would allow him access to everything but the high-roller suites without question. He changed faces again; no sense in tipping anyone off as to what he was up to, since there was always the off chance that someone watching a security cam feed was actually paying attention. Next objective was to find a terminal hooked into the hotel's registry; somewhere near the kitchen ought to work. Following his nose again combined with his knowledge of general hotel layout, it didn't take him long to find what he was looking for. The terminal was set up for the waiter staff so that they could ferry room service orders promptly to the guests. It was a closed system, which meant that it wasn't connected to any outside net. He was going to need a hand to get the information he needed out of it. Tapping his comm unit, Humph spoke in a whisper. "You still paying attention, boys? I'm in, and need you to actually earn your overly generous wages."

Jim was the first one to reply. "On it, boss. Whaddya need this time?"

The Boggart attached a miniature transceiver to the data link on the side of the terminal, checking over his shoulder as he spoke. "Need you to do a remote hack, find out which room Harry is holed up in under his fake name. Got it? Link is up and ready whenever you are."

"My magic fingers are at your command," Fred quipped, sounding actually chipper. "Oh, this is sad, sad *and* pathetic.

You're gonna need to remember this one, boss, there is no ice and no firewall from this terminal, and they left 'support' as an ID and 'guest' as a password. Amateurs. Room 1210."

"Good work." Humph retrieved the transceiver and was about to cut the comm line when that familiar feeling of unease crept into his belly and up his spine. "Do me a favor, keep digging about our employer and the mark. I've got a feeling on this one; it's been too damned easy so far."

"Bugger. I hate it when you get feelings. Are you sure it wasn't just something you ate?" By this time in their association, Fred knew very well when to trust Humph's gut. He waited a few beats, and then sighed. "Roger. Preparing for excrement to hit rotating blades. Out."

Time to figure out my next move. The room that Harry was staying in was on the high-roller level of suites, which made sense; the playboy wouldn't be caught dead in anything less, even when he was on the run. This presented a problem for Humph; that level was security-restricted, and the low-security rating RFID tags in his clothing wouldn't grant him access. *Guess I'll have to break out a moldy oldie from my bag of tricks.* Since the terminal was still open, he put in an order for room service to an occupied suite on the same level as Harry. Putting in an order to Mr. Somerfield's room might tip him off, and Humph really didn't want the aggravation of a foot chase this late in the game. Access to the level was really what he needed. Once there, Humph would have more time to observe the situation. Nine times out of ten in his job, roundabout was better than going straight to the objective. Besides, with no idea whether or not Harry was in the room, alone, with companions, or hosting a free-for-all orgy, manifesting right *there* would be a very bad idea.

After the order was completed and the terminal powered off, Humph made his way to the pickup area and waited. Just as he expected, a snooty-looking waiter arrived soon after, checking the details for the order on the terminal; Humph saw that it was for the order he had put in. Sidling up to the waiter, he used some well practiced sleight of hand to slip his pocket watch into a pocket on the waiter's jacket; a simple-brush-by was all it took—that, and a craven apology. The waiter might have looked snooty, but at least he wasn't mean to the help. "Think nothing of it," he murmured, hoisting the heavy tray up over his shoulder.

When he was sure that no one was looking, he slipped into the nowhere-space connected to his watch, and waited some more. He had called it the Between. It wasn't "like" anything at all, he had a vague idea of where the watch was going, but other than that, the closest you could come to describing what used to be the Between was that there was literally nothing to describe. But it was a great place for a nap.

Back when he had been a simple Boggart, the Between had been something else entirely. He had been tied, not to an object, his pocket watch, but to the Land, and the house on it, and to a certain extent, to the people living there. For some immortals, like the Boggart, there's no concrete Beginning; you just are. That had given him a different nature entirely, and access to more expanded powers. He had been a trickster, but one that confined his mischief to amusing or useful pranks as long as he was given his portion of what the farmer produced—usually in the form of some of the food at meals, and of the drink the farmer brewed. But most importantly, he had access to the energy the land and the people produced. And the Between, his other space, had given him immortality, let him sleep for centuries if he chose, and gave him what was, essentially, his own little world. A repository for his Power, what he drew on from the land and the people on it.

Then he'd been summoned and bound, all of his vast being forced into a tiny object, and been cut off from all of that. Now, though he didn't much like to think about it, he was no longer immortal. Long-lived, certainly, but no longer immortal. He was tied to the mortal plane. The Between had become his nowhere-space; a place of emptiness, where he could still retreat to, but not for millennia or even decades. His existence had become hollowed and terrestrial all at once. It was something he had learned to live with and, despite everything, was comfortable with now. After all, there was single malt scotch.

There was a sensation of traveling on the same level for a while, followed by the feeling of rising. While in the nowhere-space, Humph changed his face again. He was going to need a new one to retrieve the watch. When he felt that the watch was no longer rising, but moving horizontally again, he waited for a moment, then materialized about twenty feet on the back-path, behind the waiter, counting on the fact that the man would be too busy balancing the heavy tray to notice anything going on behind him. He tailed the waiter just long enough for the man to reach the appointed door, and as he started to put the tray down, Humph hurried a few steps. "Here, pal, lemme give you a hand with that," he said, retrieving his watch as he aided the waiter in dropping the tray onto a receiving table beside the door. The waiter nodded thanks, then turned to the door, using his pass-key to get in. On this level, you didn't expect to have to answer the door yourself. Humph hurried on.

That went almost too well. It'd be nice to have good luck instead of no luck to bad luck, and I'm not one to look at easy money askance. But still... Humph shrugged the feeling off, focusing his thoughts on the job at hand. It didn't take him long to find Harry's room; it was one of the larger suites and was tucked in a corner, which meant it didn't have an abundance of adjacent rooms like the smaller ones did.

Well, now he was here, so this was the sixty-four-million-credit question. Sneak in, or bust in? There was no question but that Humph was going to have to *get* in, the only real question was how. He tested the door, mostly out of reflex—and found that it swung inside easily. And that could only be bad news for Humph. *Oh, goddamnit all. I hate it when I'm right.* His belly tightened up, and the feeling of uneasiness came back with full force. He hunched down as he pushed the door all the way in, keeping behind the wall and only peeking out enough to see into the room. When no one started shooting or yelling at him, he decided it was safe enough to venture inside.

To put it plainly, the room was a mess. Most of the highly expensive wooden furniture had been overturned, some of it broken to pieces. Brocade upholstery was shredded. One of the crystal light fixtures was hanging out of the socket, flicking on and off unsteadily. The bed was torn up, with stuffing and bits of memory foam showered around it like debris from a bomb's crater. Linens with a thread-count higher than an executive's salary had been reduced to rags. Humph began to poke through the remnants of the room, toeing over piles of scattered papers or ruined silk-velvet drapes. He'd tossed a lot of rooms in his time, looking for clues or hints that would help him finish a job, and he recognized this room for what it was; a setup. Whoever had done this job wanted it to look this way, not because they were looking for anything in particular. It was painting a picture with nice broad strokes; only a critical eye would recognize it as an orchestrated scene. And with a joint with as much security as this one had, how had "they" gotten in to do this in the first place? *What in the hell is going on here? Something is way wrong with this entire gig. I'll give it one last sweep, see if I can find anything that'll point me to Harry, and then hightail it back to the office to—*

Humph froze when he heard the door squeak on its hinge, his thoughts stopped midway through. He was almost startled enough to drop the face he had glamoured on. Slowly, he turned around to face whoever was there. The man standing in the doorway, obviously drunk, was a perfect match for Harry Somerfield. Mid-30s, boyishly handsome with a hint of sleaze, tailored casual suit, and a bottle of high-end liquor in hand completed the picture.

"Uh, are you with Housekeeping?" Harry slurred, so drunk that he was momentarily oblivious to the fact that his expensive hotel room had been trashed.

Humph was about to offer a witty one-liner when he noticed two red dots circling over Harry's breast pocket. Reacting without bothering to think about it, Humph dove for Harry, tackling the drunk in a rough bear hug. Two lasers stitched the door and the wall that Harry had been standing in front of, cutting lazy lines into them and setting them on fire. The lasers stopped just as quickly and silently.

Two snipers—maybe more. I gotta figure out how many shaved monkeys are in this equation. Harry had started struggling underneath him, mumbling about paying his tab. Humph roughly shoved his head against the floor. The targeting lasers started up again, sweeping the walls of the room, looking for victims. Things immediately took a turn for the worse; at the end of the hall past the open door, Humph saw two lugs in suits round the corner. Upon spotting Humph and Harry, both began to reach inside their jackets; guessing that they weren't fumbling for their room keys, Humph reached out and slammed the now fully engulfed door shut. "Stay low if you want your head to stay attached to your shoulders!" He started to drag Harry bodily to some cover while keeping himself as low to the floor as possible; there was an overturned table near the wall with the window. Getting behind the table wouldn't give them much cover, but they'd be close enough to the wall to avoid the snipers. *One problem at a time.*

Humph had just enough time to reach into his uniform and retrieve the Webley-Fosbery revolver and peer around the edge of the table before the flaming door was kicked in. Both of the lugs had some very nasty pistols in their hands, and were scanning the room.

Somewhere in the back of his mind, part of him was facepalming. *Burning hells.* "*Two guys bust through the door, guns blazing....*" *When I catch whoever is writing my life, I'm going to feed him his liver.* The Boggart waited until one of them was distracted, talking to someone on the other end of the earpiece that he was wearing. Humph leaned out around the right side of the table, leveling the heavy revolver dead center at the thug's chest before squeezing off two rounds. The thug crumpled while his partner dove for cover. Then the thug got back *up*, shooting as he ducked behind a pillar. "Damnit! Bastards have body armor. I don't have the right bullets for this. Shitfire!" The table that Humph and Harry were hiding behind was starting to get chipped away; the thugs were methodical, if nothing else, and were working from the top to the bottom of the table with their shots.

Harry had finally started to come to; Humph found that gunfire often had a sobering effect on most beings. "W-what the hell! Who are you? Why are those guys shooting at us? Where's sec—" The Boggart smacked Harry, hard, to shut him up.

"They're trying to kill us. There are snipers outside, so we can't jump out onto the fire escape. This table isn't going to last much longer; once it goes, we're going to get turned into Swiss cheese. Any other questions?"

Harry gulped, and then nodded. "Yes. What the hell are you going to do about it!"

That's actually not a bad question. They couldn't stay here much longer; the two goons were getting cocky now, and had come out of cover to advance on the table, still firing. They were decently trained; communicating and making sure that one was covering the other when someone had to reload. Any move that Humph made would probably get him shot. He could hide in his pocket watch, but then Harry was certainly dead meat; these guys clearly wanted both of them dead. *Pocket watch...got it!* He fished the pocket watch out of the borrowed uniform, then chucked it hard over what was left of the top of the table. *I hope it went far enough, otherwise this'll have turned out to be a very bad idea.* He waited a heartbeat, went to the nowhere-space, and immediately came out of it again centered on the watch. Both of the goons were now in front of him, still working on the table with their expensive guns. Unceremoniously, Humph raised his revolver and planted a lead slug in the back of each of their heads. The goons fell to the floor like puppets with the strings cut, no time to react before they were already dead.

"Time to beat feet, Mr. Somerfield!" The snipers hadn't cut him down; they must've been confused by what had just happened. Humph knew that wouldn't last, however. He ran full tilt toward the table, ducking at the last second; a laser beam cut through the air an inch above his left ear. Humph expended the last two shots from the revolver in the general direction of the snipers; hopefully it'd give them something to think about. Without missing a beat he grabbed Harry by the collar and dragged him toward the remains of the doorway; both snipers had finally wised up and were firing in concert again.

It was all that Humph could do to keep Harry upright and moving, half dragging and half carrying him down the hallway. All the gunfire might have sobered up his head somewhat, but the rest of his body was still very drunk. Amazingly, he hadn't dropped the bottle that he had been carrying. *Time to figure out an exit strategy. I've got to get this guy back to the office and lose this heat. Why the hell haven't the security alarms gone off?* There were two most-likely answers to that; either someone had bribed hotel security to look the other way, or someone had hacked the hotel's system. Either explanation meant money, and a lot of it; places like this one didn't get cracked cheaply. This whole deal was stinking more and more the deeper he stepped in it. At least he wouldn't have to contend with innocents stepping into the line of fire. The sound-proofing in this joint was world-class. You could probably set a nuke off in the hall and no one in the rooms would hear it. They reached the elevators after what seemed like ages; Humph had to use one hand to keep Harry from toppling over while he punched the elevator controls with the grip of the revolver. Thankfully, you didn't need a key to call an elevator from this floor, the assumption being that anyone up here was supposed to be.

Those snipers wouldn't have been sitting idle; there was, without a doubt, going to be a reception committee waiting for both of them. Humph punched in the service floor; lobby was sure to be a no-go, even if the hired goons weren't there. Hotel staff were usually funny about having their customers getting dragged out by strange beings. Once the doors closed, he threw Harry up against the wall of the elevator, lifting him up by the lapels on a what had once been a very expensive jacket, before all the burn marks and tears.

"Spill it, pal. What's going on? Who has a hard on for you bad enough to send a squad of guns to grease both of us?" Humph gave him a light slap to help bring him around; instructional rather than punitive. Harry just stared at him with his mouth a little open and his eyes bulging a little.

"I—I—I—" Harry stammered. Not exactly useful. And the elevator was in "express" mode, heading straight to the service level without stopping at any other floors. The doors were going to open in a second—

Just as he thought that, the elevator slowed and stopped, and the doors whooshed smoothly open. The sight they revealed was not a pleasant one. Two out-of-breath thugs in suits, standing right at the entrance of the elevator clear as day. There was a beat where everyone just stared at each other; then everything happened at once. Both thugs started to reach for their weapons. Humph spun around, still holding onto Harry's jacket, and threw the playboy at the thugs. Reflexively, they caught him, one of them dropping his weapon in the process. Just as quickly, Humph was on them; he was out of bullets, so he pistol-whipped the one on the right, catching him in the temple. The other was trying to shove Harry off when Humph kicked his knee out; the man fell to the floor with a squeal of pain before he was silenced with a second kick to his chin. Both thugs were out, at least for a few moments. He kicked the one he had pistol whipped a few times; partly just to make sure he stayed down, and partly out of annoyance.

Harry had collapsed in a messy pile on the floor, still babbling about how he didn't know what was going on. *Dumb bastard is in shock. Can't say I blame him too much.*

Humph had a sudden flash as he manhandled Harry up off the floor. These goons hadn't been prepared for his reflexes or his strength. What did that mean? Boggarts such as himself weren't nearly as numerous as some other Paras were, so there wasn't much recognition by the average Joe. By nature his kind were solitary, and usually were tied to one place.

Well if they didn't know what he was capable of before, they were probably figuring it out now. Better take advantage of the fact while he still *had* an advantage. Rather than try and get Harry to move under his own power, Humph heaved the playboy over his shoulders in a fireman's-carry position, and sprinted for the back door. There were a few startled wait staff and other hotel employees about, but he was moving too fast and didn't look like he would brook any opposition. Having the Webley-Fosbery tucked into his waistband certainly didn't hurt that impression.

Ever the cautious one, Humph had left a rented van-pod about half a block away in an alley. Sometimes renting from Hire-A-Heap paid off, especially when you were trying to be inconspicuous; the risks you took with the vehicle in question having a motor powered by anemic hamsters were offset by the fact that it was invisible and *no one* wanted to jack it. Not worth the time or effort. The only change to the egg-shaped carrier since he'd left it was that the inevitable wag had written *Wash Me* in the dirt on the side.

The pod responded to the proximity of the key in his pocket by sliding open the cargo door. A malfunction—it was the *driver* door that was supposed to pop—but one that served his purpose better right now. He heaved Harry inside, the playboy still as limp as if he was the one who had been cold-cocked, and wrenched the driver door open.

Humph changed his face again as he climbed into the driver seat. Another one of his standbys, meant to look like any regular shmoe; easily forgettable. He also shrugged off the stolen uniform jacket, opting to throw it in the back on top of Harry. "Stay down and out of sight," he growled as he plugged the key into the dash-socket. The van thought about that key for a lot longer than he would have liked, despite having recognized it to open the door for him, but finally, and reluctantly started. *"Warning,"* said the robotic voice from the dash. *"We are in a non-controlled access-way. Vehicles will not be under auto-control."*

"No shit, Sherlock," the Boggart snarled under his breath, and hit the accelerator. The pod responded sluggishly, but did move out. At least he'd fit in with every other driver in these alleys; they *all* drove like madmen once off the traffic grid. Deliveries had to be made and every second you were late cost credits off your take-home pay. Three more pods sped toward him and scraped past him, just barely *not* hitting the wall. One rode his tail for a moment, and as soon as the way was clear, squeaked past him and accelerated. Humph wished he had *that* one right now.

The Boggart keyed his comm unit; it was set to call the office on autodial. The line rang for a good two minutes before he cut the connection. *Not good. Skinny Jim always picks up by the third ring, no exceptions. That means the office is a no-go.* He had to think fast, now; find someplace to stash the mark and collect his thoughts. He didn't have Jim and Fred to op for him, which was bad; he'd be flying blind.

You worked for years without a partner, he reminded himself. *All right, then, let's do it.* Yanking the cyclic around and peeling down an intersecting alley, he pummeled his brain for an alternate safe house.

It was close to an hour later before Humph had found the right spot to hole up in. He had driven around for a while, mostly at random, before he parked; hopefully no one who was paying attention would think that there was any pattern to what he was doing, and get a direction off of him. As stealthily as possible, he had climbed under the van-pod, poking around in its guts and desperately hoping the hover system wouldn't give out; if it did, his troubles would be over, permanently. After burning himself twice and getting a nice shock from an exposed wire, he had found what he was looking for; the GPS locator that the rental company used to keep track of its fleet. It hadn't been enabled yet; usually they only did that if there was suspicion that the vehicle had been stolen, or if the law came with a warrant. Still, Humph didn't want to take any chances, so he removed it without completely busting it. There was a parked taxi not too far away; the driver was off duty or otherwise occupied; a few more minutes of jerry-rigging, and the locator was now affixed to the frame of the cab. If anyone *did* start looking for his ride, they'd have to chase the cab around for a while before they figured out the game; might buy him a little time.

With that chore out of the way, Humph took a circuitous route to the safe house. In all actuality, it was more like a safe closet; barely big enough for the bed, sink, vidscreen and toilet. If two people wanted to pass each other, it would be a tight fit even with both turning their shoulders. Comfort wasn't why he had rented it, though; it was cheap, and in a part of town where keeping your mouth shut was often part of a long-term survival strategy. Paying in cash and slipping a couple hundred extra to the building super sealed the deal; discretion, aided by another forgettable face and a fake name.

Stashing the van-pod down the street, Humph resigned himself to lugging Harry to the apartment. *Across the street and up three flights of stairs. My day keeps getting better and better.* If anyone asked, he figured that he could get away with saying that he was helping his friend who had drunk too much to get home. It would even be partly true, after all. Harry *was* drunk, and had passed out. Around here, he imagined that it wouldn't be an uncommon sight. After an agonizing climb, he had finally managed to get Harry to the apartment, plop him on the bed, lock all of the security devices on the door, and slump to the cheap carpeting next to the sink. He was almost desperately grateful that if he needed to—and he probably would—he could retreat to his watch to escape Harry. And Harry's snoring. Harry was a world-class snorer. And somehow still had that bottle clenched in his paw; empty now, probably poured out in their flight from the hotel.

The Boggart sat there for a few minutes, staring at the wall and catching his breath. The adrenaline had finally worn off, and he felt like he was another couple of hundred years older. Tiredly, he fumbled under the sink until his fingers wrapped around a roughly cylindrical object. *Thanks be for small favors.* A small bottle of single malt scotch was taped and stashed under the sink. Uncorking it with his teeth, Humph took a belt from it. And then another. In a few moments, the bottle was half empty, but the Boggart didn't even feel a buzz, just a marginal relaxation and warmth spreading from his middle outward. Adrenaline—or whatever it was in his system that passed for it—had eaten most of the effect. *Now I can think.*

The absolute last thing that the Boggart expected was for the landline phone to ring. It took him a moment, but he realized that it wasn't his comm unit. That's when the stab of fear hit him, for the first time. It was the phone line for the safe house; all these rooms had an old-fashioned phone, the sort of arrangement that someone who didn't want his conversations out on the airwaves to picked up by anyone with the proper equipment appreciated. No one, not even Jim and Fred, had this number. The line kept ringing, persistently.

Slowly, the Boggart picked up the receiver for it, his mouth dry before he breathed, "Hello?"

"Hello, Mr. Boggart."

Humph put some steel in his voice. "Who is this?"

"I represent parties that are interested in offering you a one-time-only deal. It will not be repeated after this communication, and there will be no junctures for future communication." The voice had been run through an anonymizer. Every possible inflection had been taken out. Robots sounded more human than this.

"What's the deal?" Caution was in order here. Whoever it was had somehow tracked him down and knew where he was and that he had Harry. That in and of itself was no mean feat; Humph was pretty damned good at what he did, and no one should have been able to find him here at this safe house. Which meant whoever it was probably had the ability to do whatever he said he could do.

"Give us Mr. Somerfield. You'll be able to walk away from this, free and clear, and be given a very large remuneration for your troubles thus far."

Humph was silent for a moment, weighing the offer. "And if I don't give him to you?"

"The alternative will be…unpleasant."

That means they'll kill me. Humph thought it through. The kid was nothing to him; he didn't know him, and it wasn't like he owed him anything, much less his life. Whoever was after the kid was serious about getting him; they were willing to kill, but also willing to throw large bundles of money at the problem if that's what it took. This case had already turned out to be more of a headache than it was worth; if he took this deal and whoever was offering it kept their end of it, he could get away clean with a stack of cash. It was a good play; even if the other side didn't honor their arrangement, he still had a better shot of living through the situation if he didn't have the kid around.

There was another voice, no less clear, that told him he wasn't going to take the deal. These pricks had tried to kill him, as a matter of course. Humph usually didn't let little things like that slide. Attempts on his life pissed him off, if nothing else. It was bad for business, too; no use letting it get around that just anyone could decide to take him down. The more he thought about it, the more he decided that he wanted to find out why someone had figured bumping him off was a good idea. Besides, he had taken a job; he'd signed on the proverbial dotted line, accepted the first payment. Once he was bought, it was a point of honor with him to stay bought. He wasn't just "a Boggart," he was "*the* Boggart" for a damned good reason; when he took a job, it got done, no matter what.

"The answer is no."

"Very well." The line disconnected with a click.

The Boggart sat there wondering if he had just made a huge mistake; in any case, it was too late now. He was going to have to follow this line to the end.

He tried the office again. Nada. A very, very bad sign. A sign that the Boggart and his firm had both been set up. He turned on the vidscreen, keeping the volume low, and keyed in the Crime Channel, which showed rolling live reports of criminal activity based on your area. Immediately he knew that all of his fears were justified.

"*...a heinous deed has taken place not more than two hours ago. We're here at the scene where the police are busy interviewing witnesses and sending in crime scene investigators. It appears that we have another in the latest rash of Para-on-Human violence; a local Boggart has been implicated in the kidnapping of one Harry Somerfield, the heir to Somerfield Botanicals. From what our sources have divulged, the Boggart in question stormed Mr. Somerfield's room, killing two of his security detail and subduing two others before abducting him. Police state that the office which is the Boggart's only known address has been raided, but*" *there was no sign of where the Boggart, Mr. Somerfield, or any accomplices are. Police ask for the help of the community for any information—"*

Humph shut off the vidscreen in disgust. *Well, fuck.* There was no doubt about it now; he was being framed, and the setup had maybe been in place from the get-go, somehow. This sort of frame job didn't just happen in the blink of an eye; a not-so-insignificant amount of prep work had gone into this. Those goons had been trying to kill both of them, not to mention the snipers that had done their level best to make mincemeat out of Harry from the opener; no way were they part of any "security detail." The newsfeed didn't bode well for Fred and Jim, either; if the cops had them, it would have said so. They were probably either dead or taken by whoever was behind this cluster. Maybe, *maybe,* they had gotten away, but if they had, they were in the wind and might as well be dead, for all the help they would be; the "lifeguard's rule" of "you have to save yourself first" was one all three of them knew well. Everything was swirling around in his mind, and the Boggart was getting more and more pissed off with each passing second. *It's time for some goddamned answers.* He took another quaff of whisky, then stood up and stomped over to the bed. Harry was just starting to come to.

The Boggart roughly yanked Harry up, pinning him against the wall. He caught movement in the corner of his eye, and leaned out of the way as Harry swung the empty bottle at his head. He swatted it out of the playboy's grasp, then gave him another light slap. "Only one sheet in the wind's eye instead of all three now, huh? It's time to talk, Harry."

Harry's eyes went wide as they focused on Humph's face. "Hey, wait a minute! Who are you? Where'd the other guy go? Are you one of the guys trying to kill me?"

Humph realized he was wearing a different face than the one that Harry had met him wearing. *Whoops. Well, this ought to finish sobering him up.* He smiled…and then allowed *his* face to show, dropping the glamour. In the time it takes to blink an eye, Harry went from looking at the face of a boringly average human male to one that had a slightly feral cast, was black as coal, partially covered with short bristly fur, and had *very* sharp teeth in its smile. "Hi there, Harry. I'm the guy that saved your bacon back at the hotel. Meet the real me."

Harry's knees buckled; he only remained standing because Humph was holding him against the wall. "Wh-who are you? Why w-were you after me?"

"My name is Humphrey; just call me Humph. I was hired to find you by a tight-ass named Bevins; he seems to be under the impression that your mother cares about your half-in-the-bag ass and wants you back." He let one hand off of Harry, putting up his index finger with the claw at the end of it rather close to Harry's nose. "Now that we're properly introduced, I've got some questions for you, Harold. I'm tired and more than a little pissed off, so I'd strongly suggest that you answer truthfully and quickly."

Harry, eyes still bugged wide-open and glued on the tip of Humph's claw, nodded vigorously.

"Good. I'm glad that we understand each other. First things first: Do you know those goons in the suits, the ones that were trying to shuffle both of us off this mortal coil?" Harry shook his head, meeting Humph's eyes. "All right. Do you have any clue as to why somebody would want to kill you?" Harry gulped audibly and shook his head again. "Strike one, asshole." Humph slammed him against the wall, hard, and then brought the claw back up. "It's your neck on the line, get it, jerk? More importantly, it's my ass, too. And I'm not in any particularly big hurry to get scragged. So, let's try this again. Why are there some heavily armed lugs trying to kill us?"

Harry shook his head again, holding his hands up in front of himself defensively. "Honest, I don't know! I don't know why somebody would want me dead!"

"Then why are you on the run, chump?"

"On the run?' Harry looked at him quizzically. "I'm not on the run. Who told you that?"

Humph pushed him back up against the wall again. "I'm asking the questions right now. If you're not on the run, why the prepaid cred cards, switching hotels, and all the trouble?"

Harry started shaking like a leaf in the wind, and tried to make appeasing gestures with trembling hands. "All right, all right, take it easy. It's just kind of my thing. With that moron Bevins always snooping around for Mother, it's hard for a guy like me to have fun. Especially my kind of fun." He shrugged, looking sheepish. "So I sneak out a couple of times a month to go slumming. I use those cards and stuff to keep Bevins from reporting back exactly what I'm spending my money on; I'd get cut off if Mother knew that I was still doing it. As for the hotels, a lot of the establishments on this wretched mudball are rather draconian when it comes to their policy on escorts—"

"Okay, save it. I don't need all of the gory details on what you do between the sheets." *There's something more to this, there has to be. I've gotta keep digging.* "You're a rich kid, so kidnapping and ransom might've been a good fit if it weren't for the fact that they were trying to carve you up the same as me, earlier. And this is too elaborate of a setup if someone was just trying to bump you off as part of a corporate rivalry deal. You must have pissed someone off somewhere down the line. Welched on a bet, or more than one? Got debts? Hit on the wrong man's girl?"

"Seriously, I don't know! The worst trouble I've been in is getting thrown in the drunk tank a few times and wrecking a few hotel rooms!"

The Boggart frowned. Something had to start adding up. "What about Bevins? He's got a part in this, somehow. He hired me, set me on you. Someone would have to know that he did that, then get the cops to go along with the frame job. That takes time and money."

Harry looked around, searching for how to answer when his face went still; something had clicked for him. "Oh, god. They found out. That contemptuous bastard found out." He was talking to himself at this point. "But no, there's no way Mother would ever...would she? Let him kill me?"

Humph shook Harry. "Would you like to share with the class, sport? I don't like being held in suspense."

He looked at Humph again, his jaw somewhere in the vicinity of his ankles. "I-I stole. From the company. Well, one of the companies; just a small branch that no one pays attention to. I thought that no one would notice."

"You were skimming from your mother's company?"

"Hey, I've got needs! And Mother could cut off my allowance any time she feels like it. It was just for some extra walking-around money, honest!"

Humph sighed heavily. "Here's what's going to happen. I'm going to let go of you, and you're going to sit down on the bed and behave. You're not going to do something stupid like try and run, right? It'd turn out painful for you and exhausting for me. Know this; people in this neighborhood ignore screams on general principle. OK?" Harry looked longingly at the door, but then nodded in resignation. Humph relaxed his grip on him, and he gloomily plodded the two steps over to the foot of the bed, sitting down hard. Humph took two steps of his own over to the sink, sitting down next to it and retrieving the bottle of single malt. He took a long pull from it and waited for several long moments before he started speaking. "So, let me put all of this together. You're unhappy with whatever exorbitant amount of money that you get from your ma, so you start stealing a little extra on the side. Bevins finds out, tells her, and waits for you to go on one of your little trips. He hires me under the pretense of finding you to bring home, while he sets up an ambush to kill us both and pin the blame on me. That sound like the size of things?" He took another drink before passing the bottle to Harry. Harry shrugged disconsolately before accepting the whisky.

"I don't think Mother would ever try to have me killed. She's been disappointed in me before, but this…"

"No, there's something more to this. I don't buy it; it's too much trouble for a punk like you, especially for what would probably be a trifling amount to your sort. How much did you steal, anyways?"

Harry swallowed a mouthful of whisky, coughing roughly. "Just a couple of mil. It was for kicks, mostly."

"Yeah, that's not enough for this kind of trouble. There's something else going on." He held his hand out for the bottle, taking another drink. "I knew I shouldn't have taken this damned job; however hard up we were for money before, we sure as shit are worse off now."

They sat there in silence for a long time, passing the bottle back and forth between the two of them. Harry was the first one to speak, almost sheepish. "So…Humph, right?" The Boggart nodded. "What are you going to do?"

Humph took another long drink, finishing off the bottle. "My office is torn up. Both of my partners are either dead, snatched by the goons, or on the run. You and I have all sorts of trouble on our heels, from cops with itchy trigger fingers to thugs in suits with expensive toys. And we have next to jack and shit in creds or other resources." He stood up, dropping the empty bottle in the sink. "I aim to get to the bottom of this barrel of crap, and figure out who *exactly* dipped me in it. The who and the why of it, Harry. And you're going to help me." He held out his hand. "And to start with, you can hand over your wallet."

So far as resources went, things were looking up. One compartment of Harry's wallet was *stuffed* with prepaid credit keys; when the Boggart asked why there were so many, he had just shrugged and said, "When they get down to a couple hundred, I just stash them in the pocket and forget about them unless I need to pay a cab. Then I just give him the whole chip. Easier that way."

Everything besides the cash wasn't looking so hot. Humph only had a couple of disguises with him, all still in the van-pod. He could scrounge and come up with stuff on the fly if he had to, but he usually liked to have more options, especially if he was going to be heading into unknown territory. He didn't have any of his usual array of gadgets that might help him out, either; stuff that Jim and Fred had bought off the shelf or doctored up on their own. Humph was used to working without them, but some of those gizmos could be mighty handy. His silver knuckles were still in his coat; you never knew when you'd be running into trouble involving Weres. Lastly, there was the ammunition for his revolver. He only had two speed loaders on him for the Webley-Fosbery; one that was regular plain-jane hollow points, while the other held specialty rounds. Humph had personally hand-loaded that last set; he called them "all-sorts" bullets. *"They have a little bit of something for everyone."* They came in handy when he was dealing with some of the more exotic denizens of this universe. There was a little ammo stored at the hideout, but they probably wouldn't be able to buy much ammo while on the run; all of the government-owned gun shops would be on the lookout for them, and everyone else would be looking at the two of them like they were steak dinner due to the reward that was no doubt attached for turning them in. Well, Humph, anyway. For Harry...well, if Humph's gut instinct was right, there was a bounty on Harry, not a reward. That'd be something for headhunters, though; maybe a few dirty cops moonlighting as button men thrown in for variety.

And they were going to have to get out of here pretty quickly. It was unlikely that the goons after Harry would mount a daylight raid on this place, but the clock was ticking.

He counted up the credit keys again. *Must be nice to be rich.* Humph had an application on his comm unit that let him scan keys for the total still on them; it was useful in his line of work. And Harry was an even bigger chump than Humph had thought. Most of those keys had not a couple hundred but a couple *thousand.* Harry must have left a lot of satisfied cabbies in his wake. That would pay for a lot of low-rent rooms, food-cart meals, and transport. He wondered if Harry had ever been on commuter transit. And if he could be trusted to keep his trap shut about the heat, the smell, and the crowding.

Well, for now, they still had the van-pod. After he knew what they had to work with—and Humph had confiscated most of the keys so even if Harry pulled a runner and got away, the Boggart would still have some resources—it was on to the next stage. Because they couldn't sit in this room, eating roach-coach meals and staring at the vidscreen, for-ever. Sooner rather than later, Harry would get over being scared of the Boggart, and start bitching because he'd never been in a capsule hotel before. And after about an hour of the rich bastard's whining, Humph probably *would* kill him.

Humph had gone through his address book—he was old-fashioned; he actually kept his contacts in a little, physi-cal notebook, though it was digital storage rather than paper pages—about twenty times before he finally decided which favor he was going to call in. After a good long ponder, and checking things as best he could without triggering any alerts, he decided that it was probably safe to use the van-pod one last time. He'd have to ditch it after that though. Harry balked at the prospect of riding in it again; appar-ently he had been sick in it during their first trip. *Tough luck, Harry.* Humph made the concession of placing some old newspapers on top of the mess before he shoved Harry in. He then changed faces again before starting the cantanker-ous vehicle up.

He left it three blocks from the destination, and Harry was beginning to look decidedly put out by the fact that he was expected to *walk*. He kept his mouth shut, though, which was showing more smarts than the Boggart expected out of him. It might have been because the few denizens of the area that they passed looked as mean and dangerous as Humph—and a good half of them were Paras. Furs, mainly, identifiable by their tribal-motif clothing, themed to their species; leather, spikes, and chains, most of it easily removable in case they Were'd out. The duo kept to the alleys as much as possible, with Humph trailing Harry to keep an eye on him until they reached the last gulf of empty space between them and their destination: the back door of The Beau Bayou Club.

It was clearly a happening night; Humph could see the tail end of the line to get into the club, even from all the way over where they were. Looking both ways down the street, he spent several minutes scrutinizing the area for any stakeouts or other surveillance. Getting careless at any point could get him killed in a hurry. Harry, too. And he needed Harry alive if he wanted even a slim chance of figuring this mess out. Either Harry was the best bald-faced liar in the world (doubtful), able to keep his facade up while three-fourths drunk and entirely beaten up (even more doubtful) or he was more important than he appeared. In the Boggart's world, that usually meant he knew something. Information—the right information—was usually a thousand times more valuable than money, and the easiest way to get rid of information was to kill all of the people that possessed it.

Satisfied that they weren't going to be immediately surrounded and gunned down as soon as they crossed the street, Humph motioned for Harry to follow him. They walked casually across the street, staying a few feet apart. Humph's senses were on high alert for even the slightest thing out of the ordinary. They reached the back door without incident. There was one thing out of place, however; a surveillance camera was panning back and forth over the top of the door. Once they got close, it stopped, then zoomed in on Humph. *Hm. He must be getting paranoid in his old age.*

Now we see if my old code still works. It had been a long time since he'd used the back door of the Beau Bayou, and back then it had been because of a dame. Still, the dame hadn't been *his*, the affair had been resolved thanks to his intervention to the satisfaction of all parties, so…

He punched in the numbers, and heard the *hum, click* of the electronic lock on the door opening. The Boggart ushered Harry in, closing the door behind them. They were in darkness for a few moments before Humph took Harry by the arm and started leading him down the dim hallway they had found themselves in. There was faint red lighting as they moved forward, the smell of spicy food, and loud music thumping through the walls. At the end of the hallway was a large black door; it had a life-sized embossed skeleton in a top hat on it. Humph turned to Harry. "Whatever happens on the other side of this door, you stick close to me. Got it?" Harry nodded. Then he nearly jumped out of his skin when the skeleton talked.

"Who's your date, Boggart? Not your usual fare." The skeleton shifted in the door, and uttered a dry chuckle. "Never pictured you as a switch-hitter."

"Can it, Happy, otherwise I'll make a xylophone out of your ribcage." They waited for a few tense moments. "Well, are you gonna let us in?"

The skeleton seemed to grin wider. "Password, please?"

"For the love of—" Humph fumed. "'You're pretty humerus, Happy.'"

Harry looked from the Boggart to the skeleton with a vaguely disgusted expression. "Seriously? A bone pun?"

The skeleton cackled; it sounded like a bad wind chime with all of its ribs clacking together. "You and your girlfriend can pass, Boggart. But watch out; they'll eat your date alive in there. Got some bad actors for customers tonight."

The door opened by itself. Given its skeletal passenger, it might have been expected to creak ominously, but it was silent—the kind of silence only a lot of money can buy. The loud, thumping music stopped a second or two after the door closed behind them, giving way to something more subdued. The Boggart very much doubted that Harry would have identified either piece—the first had been a loud, brassy number in the New Orleans jazz tradition; the second was also jazz, but cool Chicago-style. Not that one customer in a hundred would know the difference, nor that you'd have risked getting stoned to death in a New Orleans jazz club for playing Chicago tunes. The Boggart opened another door at the end of the hallway, and they walked into the club proper.

It was dark. Most of the lighting was from flickering pseudo-candles on the tables. Overhead, the ceiling had been done with a real-to-life nightscape, showing more stars than you would ever see on an overcast New Orleans night. The walls were made to look like rough timber, as if this was a jazz-joint from about the turn of the 20th century. The rest of the lighting wasn't coming from any obvious source, but pools of red radiance as dark as blood splashed across everything. They started to pick their way through the crowd, weaving up to the bar. And what a crowd it was; Happy wasn't kidding when he warned that some of the patrons might fancy eating Harry alive.

Most obvious were the Fangs and Furs; some of the latter actually wore the teeth and claws of vanquished rivals as trophies. But there were some truly strange Paras that were regulars at this club as well; they edged past a table where a human-headed, lion-bodied androsphinx was sipping a mint julep and discussing something with a Jersey Devil. A Bigfoot loomed over the end of one of the three bars around the room. A gorgeous woman in a flowing white dress and blonde hair down to her ankles smiled at Harry, and the Boggart had to grab his elbow and shake it before he did something stupid. The next moment, though, his own good sense—or what passed for it—kicked in, as the woman turned away, revealing that her body was hollow from the rear, as if she was only half of a display mannequin, which was certainly enough weirdness to make Harry back off even if he didn't know what that meant.

The regular customers of the Beau Bayou were...the deadly sorts of Paras. Most of them were kept in check by the legal system...or by being careful where they picked their victims. They all came here originally for different reasons, but kept coming back for the same one: Whatever you wanted, you could probably find, buy, or arrange to have stolen at the Beau Bayou. There were Norms here, too: the usual assortment of Fang and Fur groupies, who wisely chose to stay close to whomever they were fawning over. But there were others, as well; anyone that might have dealings with Paras that wouldn't bear the light of day was here, wheeling and dealing with everyone else.

And then there was the bartender at the main bar—the one that the Bigfoot was bookending. As tall as the Bigfoot or a fully wolfed-out Were, the Rougarou had a heavily muscled humanoid torso, humanoid hands ending in claws, the head of a wolf, and literally glowing red eyes. He had a beard as well, neatly braided and finished off with a gold ring, and a very expensive silk brocade vest over a red silk shirt. Presumably he was wearing equally expensive trousers as well, but his lower half was hidden by the bar. Probably just as well. The Boggart really did not *want* to know whether or not he was wearing pants.

The Rougarou noticed Humph and Harry as they reached the bar, stomping over after refilling the Bigfoot's bowling-ball-sized goblet. "Humph, long time no see." Humph knew that the bartender had an extremely rare and ridiculously expensive anti-glamor charm, which was how he was able to recognize any previous but englamored customer on sight. He sniffed, then looked over at Harry. "Who's the appetizer?"

"Nice to see you, too, Alphonse. And he's a client. Where's—"

Humph—and nearly everyone else in the club—stopped in the middle of what they were doing and looked toward the stage. A new song had begun; this one had a singer who had just begun vocalizing. Now *every* head was turned her way.

She was as blonde as the hollow woman had been, with her long hair done up loosely on the top of her head in a way that somehow made Humph's fingers itch to find the pins that held it in place and let it fall down around her. Big blue eyes that should have looked innocent, and instead looked sleepily sensuous, dominated a heart-shaped face. Her neck was a long ivory sweep, her body, in a tight-fitting black beaded gown, was made of curves, and she moved like the wind on the water as she sang.

Humph couldn't have said *what* she was singing—blues, maybe. He didn't recognize the song, and anyway the song was irrelevant compared to the singing. Her voice was like velvet, or cream with a touch of whiskey, and the words didn't matter at all. Every word held an unspoken promise, and he knew everyone else was hearing the same promise that he was. Of course they did. This was a Lorelei—the German version of a siren—and although she wasn't luring men to their deaths on the rocks of her river, there were still plenty of rocks to run aground on if you tried to make her hold good to the promise the melody was holding just out of reach.

Her eyes moved slowly over the crowd, until she reached the part where the Boggart and his charge were standing. And her eyes passed over Harry as if he wasn't there and locked with Humph's.

For a moment it felt as if he had grabbed live wires in either hand.

Then the song ended, the moment passed, and she dropped her gaze before starting another number. Everyone in the club waited a few heartbeats before they resumed what they had been doing. A few threw wistful or irritated looks over at Humph; clearly something had happened and they felt cheated that it had happened to *him* but not *them*.

He shook himself out of it. The spell, or whatever the hell it was, was over. He tried to look around the crowd to see the singer, but everyone was suddenly in the way. Harry tugged at his arm impatiently; a couple of the patrons were starting to leer at him, licking their chops. Humph turned back to Alphonse, still feeling slightly inebriated from the last song. "Anyways, where's the boss? I need words with him."

Alphonse had his lips curled up in a wicked grin; maybe it was just the only way that he could smile, but Humph still hated it. "He's working the crowd; got some new customers in tonight and he wants to make sure they feel at home." The grin broadened. "But not *so* much at home that they get out of hand, if you know what I mean." He pointed the glass that he was cleaning over Humph's shoulder; he turned to look, and there was the man of the hour himself.

Jeanpaul Beausolei had owned the Beau Bayou for as long as anyone on-planet could remember. It seemed that he and the club had just sprung up one day, and been a landmark for the planet ever since. He styled himself as a retired voodoo priest; no one had really tried to challenge that claim. At least, no one who had lived to talk about it afterward. He had a theatrical personality—or at least a theatrical persona—and themed his in-public look to match his bar. It didn't hurt that he was almost eight feet tall, either. If he was a Para, he wasn't a sort that the Boggart recognized, and he hadn't revealed what sort he was. On the other hand, if he *wasn't* a Para, the Boggart wasn't sure how he had managed to keep the Bayou going without incident all these years. A lot of Paras still respected sheer might; he with the biggest fangs and claws and the willingness to use them ruled.

Making his way genially through the crowd was a dusky-skinned, apparently human man; his natural height was exaggerated by the tall and flawless black silk top hat he wore, complete with a silk ribbon rose tacked to the hatband. Beneath the hat, he was bald. The hat was matched with a silk tuxedo, also black, the sort with a cutaway jacket and tails. But under the jacket, instead of the usual white tux shirt, was a vest brocaded with skulls and a blood red shirt with a ruffled jabot. The ruffled cuffs of the shirt peeked out from the end of the jacket's sleeves. Jeanpaul carried a cane matched to his height that appeared to have a snake carved coiled up its length. That was only an appearance; the snake was real, and alive, and had been known to slither up the cane and down Jeanpaul's hand to partake of his drink.

And when he turned his head, just right, to just the perfect angle, it looked as if there was nothing but a skull where his face ought to be. The Boggart had never been able to work out if that was a magical illusion, some sort of hologram, or a hint at Jeanpaul's real nature; it served to creep damn near everyone out, however, which he suspected was its sole purpose.

Currently he had two nymph waitresses with flowers in their hair hanging on either arm; goblet of wine in one hand, his cane in the other. Evidently he wasn't interested in sharing with his snake tonight. He was flamboyantly entertaining a mixed group of Paras and Norms, all of whom seemed enraptured by his every word. This went on for several minutes, with Jeanpaul bouncing from clique to clique, keeping everyone happy and feeling like they were special guests.

He really does know how to work a room, I'll give him that much.

Not once during his circuit did Jeanpaul come near or even acknowledge that Humph and Harry were there. Humph went ahead and ordered a couple of drinks for them; he hardly touched his, instead looking around for the singer again. Finally, when Jeanpaul was done schmoozing, he sent the two waitresses scurrying off while he retired to the back room. Less than a minute later a very tired looking satyr, another one of the wait staff, approached them.

"Mr. Beausolei would like it if you two gentlemen would share a drink in his office, if you please." The Boggart knew that was an order framed as a request, even if Harry was oblivious to the fact. Not for the first time, Humph wondered how Harry had survived as long as he had without losing life, a limb, or at least teeth. *Fortuna favet fatuis, I guess.* Or maybe it was the insulating cocoon that money wrapped around the rich. They followed the satyr through the crowd toward the back; Harry stepped on a few toes, hooves, and other unidentifiable appendages on the way, much to the displeasure of their owners. They came to the door, where the satyr turned and left them. It opened, this one again doing so without the apparent help of anyone. Jeanpaul was seated at a large polished ebony desk; his frame made it seem like a toy in comparison. He gestured for them to come inside, with the door shutting firmly behind. For a moment, Humph was disturbingly reminded of a certain "interview" with a Wendigo that had taken place in a similar setting.

"Why lookie what have come to me humble establish-*ment*, but Mister Boggie himself! Been an age, has it not?"

"You know that you sound like you're half-Jamaican out there, Paulie. Layin' it on a bit thick tonight, aren't you?" Humph softened the criticism with a lopsided smile.

Jeanpaul smiled even wider. "Half of the rubes out there wouldn't know a New Orleans native if one was crawling up their leg and gnawing on them. How've you been, Humph?" The thick accent was gone now; Jeanpaul's voice was deeper and mellow, with just a tinge of the American South in it.

"Been better." Jeanpaul reacted to this statement by reaching under his desk, pulling out two glasses full of ice, and placing them across from the Boggart and Harry. Next to come from under the desk was an unlabeled bottle of dark, viscous liquid, which he poured for both of them. Humph's nose told him it was Paulie's privately-made rum—made as it had been in the Caribbean centuries ago, from sugar-cane molasses.

"You don't say? Been a long time since you last made the news. Now you're all that anyone can talk about. If you were wearing your own face out there, I have no doubt that some nasty so and so's would be very happy to sell your whereabouts in the time it'd take you to blink." He held up a hand. "No need to worry about anything from my staff; they know which side their bread is buttered on. No one will go out to cause you any trouble, not here."

"Good to see that some things never change. Things have become…complicated, for me. I didn't kidnap this lump. Well, not technically, at least." Harry looked up from the rum, waving shyly to Jeanpaul. "The news-feed is being doctored. I'll let you draw your own conclusions about how deep I am in it."

Jeanpaul appraised both of them. "You'd need a really tall ladder just to climb to the bottom of the shit barrel that the two of you are in right now." He paused, turning his head. "That's why you're here, right?"

Humph nodded. "That's about the size of it, Paulie. I need some breathing room; I figure getting off-planet will help with that, give me some room to move and try to figure this mess out." He sipped his rum, jerking a thumb over to Harry. "There's something bad surrounding ol' Harold here, and I'm caught in it whether I like it or not. You're just about the only person I know that can get both of us off this rock without tipping things to the bulls."

"You're right about that, Humph. You've made more than your fair share of enemies over the years; there are a lot of beings out there who would love to see you crash and burn in the worst way. You don't think this is that, do you? Someone settling old scores?"

He shook his head, swirling the rum a little in his glass as he thought. "No, it doesn't fit. There's a lot easier and messier ways to get that done, and this doesn't have the fingerprints of any of the usual suspects. Besides, why involve the rich kid in it? That complicates things way too much. On the other hand, if you figure I was set up to be the fall guy for taking the rich kid out of the picture, it all makes way too much sense." The Boggart finished his rum, setting the empty glass down on the desk. "What do you think, Paulie? All debts are paid if you can help me out of this jam."

Jeanpaul had brought his snake-cane over, allowing it to drink a little from his glass. "Your 'client' there is going along with all of this?"

Harry started to speak up before Humph cut him off. "He doesn't have any choice in the matter. He's as good as dead on his own; the lad is really like a babe in the woods. Besides, I have need of him. Only way that I'm going to be able to get to the bottom of things is using him."

"Fair enough." He looked at both of them, pondering the situation. "Very well, you've convinced me, ol' buddy. It isn't going to be easy, but I think we can work something out. I know a guy who runs a trans-orbital garbage scow for a service. Something that'll get you off of dirtside, and will bypass a lot of the usual checks and searches." He leaned back in his chair. "Meanwhile, you relax. I'll have the kitchen send in a meal. Just let Jeanpaul do the heavy lifting."

"Thanks for this, Paulie. I meant it when I said we're square after this is done—"

The Boggart stopped halfway through his sentence. From the main room, he could hear that the band had stopped playing. There was shouting and other sounds of a commotion out there, and that sick feeling had returned to his stomach.

Jeanpaul frowned, and took a firm grip on his cane. "Well, drat. They're a mite early."

The Boggart stared daggers at the club owner. "You goddamned rat. You've sold me out."

"Economics, Humph. It was you or my bar, and there's no way I'm letting anyone take *my bar.*" He spread his hands, looking apologetic. "Just the way it is." *Someone's leaning on Jeanpaul? That...has never happened before.*

Humph turned to the door for a moment, reaching for his revolver. "Forget what I said about scores, Paulie, 'cause now I owe you big—" When he turned back, Jeanpaul was gone, vanished into thin air. *Slippery bastard.*

Harry had dropped his glass, his eyes as big as saucers. "What are we going to do? There's no way out of this room except for the way we came in!"

"We can't stay here, that much is for certain. Come on, and keep your head down. It sounds like it's going to be messy out there." Humph thought for a moment, making sure that his revolver was loaded; the regular hollow points would have to do. He went for the door, opening it slightly. What he saw looked like the inside of a prison riot, or an insane asylum. *All right, Boggart. Whatever you do, don't shoot any cops.* Right now he was just the easy target for a lazy investigator. If he shot a cop or, worse, killed one, there was no place in the 'verse far enough away for him to hide. Cops were really persistent when it came to tracking down and "dealing" with those who had killed one of their own. They were the biggest and baddest gang out there, when you got right down to it, and their style of retribution wasn't exactly a short or pretty process.

The first thing that stood out was that there were a *lot* of cops. And more were trying to pour in through the front door. Everyone else in the place was either scrambling for an exit or fighting with the cops. The latter group must have thought that they were the ones that the police had come for; and this wasn't the sort of demographic that was accustomed to backing down from a fight. The Weres were sticking together; some had partially wolfed out, and were moving as small packs as they descended on targets. A few of the cops were also Weres, so whenever the two groups met a furball took place. The band was mostly cowering behind their instruments, the singer nowhere in sight. The Jersey Devil was running around, screaming wildly, and generally being in the way. Some of the Fangs had left, while others saw this as an opportune time to get some "fresh food" off the books, going after other patrons and cops alike.

Through all of this violence and bloodshed the Bigfoot was still at the end of the bar, drinking disconsolately. A bottle flew through the air and exploded on the door just above the Boggart's head. *Bar looks good right about now.* Ducking low and making sure that Harry followed him, Humph dashed over to the bar, diving behind it. Alphonse was still there; any time someone was thrown over the counter, he grabbed them and threw them right back. He looked like he was having a merry old time. After grabbing a cop and a Were in each hand and throwing them back into the fray, he looked down long enough to notice the duo. "Humph! Having fun yet?"

"What're you smiling about, you damned jackal?" Humph peeked over the edge, trying to look for a way out that wouldn't involve having to kill anyone.

"Because after this is all over with, I have to clean the joint up. And after a fracas like this, there's always lots of spilled blood." Alphonse licked his lips in anticipation, clearly savoring the meal that he would get later. "Sometimes, there are even body parts. And here I was, feeling sorry for myself because I forgot to pack a lunch."

He grabbed Alphonse by the wrist, hard, to get his attention. "Did you know that Paulie was setting me up?"

Alphonse sneered, jerking his arm away. "Please. You're assuming he'd tell any of the staff the time of day, much less that he was about to feed someone like you to the sharks. We're all mushrooms here, Boggart. He keeps us in the dark and feeds us bullshit."

Humph waited a beat, then decided he believed the bartender. He turned to Harry, grabbing him by the collar. "We're going to try for the back door. Don't get lost in this mess; if you do you might end up on Alphonse's plate. Got it?"

Harry nodded emphatically.

"Let's do it." Humph led the way, staying low. He shoved and kicked his way through, knocking a few hysterical Were groupies down here, bumping "into" the back of the hollow woman there. And it was a damn good thing that he was another Para, because he could *feel* her magic trying to suck him in, to integrate a mortal soul into her body. He wrenched himself away. Another narrow miss from a swung bottle, followed by a direct hit to the back of his head from a flying one.

"Sonofabitch!" The pain startled him more than anything, but it was enough; his glamour dropped right as he came face to face with a cop. The cop's eyes went wide with recognition. *Shit.* The cop was the first to react; he had a truncheon and apparently knew how to use it. He swung hard and fast for Humph, missing his jaw by an inch. Humph closed the distance; any blows the cop would be able to land would have that much less power that way. The cop responded by backing up and swinging wide, forcing the Boggart back. This exchange went on for a few more beats until the Boggart ducked one roundhouse swing; instead of connecting with the Boggart's temple as the cop had intended, it smashed into the nose of an already blood-crazy Fang. A trickle of blood escaped the Fang's nose as he calmly turned his head to look at the cop; he then shrieked and leapt upon the poor bastard. As the Fang sank his teeth into the cop's neck, three of the cop's compatriots piled on the Fang, hosing the whole area down with garlic-spray and using wooden truncheons on the Fang's head. The anti-Para press was going to have a field day with this entire story.

Humph moved on; it was slow going. The club had been packed before the cops barged in, and the fighting wasn't helping matters. Harry was still in tow, however. Humph tried to keep from becoming entangled in any scraps, but a very pissed-off-looking gargoyle wasn't having any of it. He had been keeping a space around himself relatively clear by thrashing his tail and knocking over anyone that got too close. Harry, too busy looking over his shoulder at another part of the fray, stepped on the gargoyle's tail, causing it to howl in rage. The gargoyle was ready to take Harry's head off when Humph stepped in; the Para focused his ire on the new target. Humph didn't want to give him any time to work up a head of steam, so he swept out one of his legs, hoping to topple him. The gargoyle simply used his tail to keep himself upright, looking vicious and smug. Humph, feeling exasperated, kicked the gargoyle square in the chest, sending it tumbling backwards into a table. The table had been occupied by a party of cyclopes, who had been staying out of the affray and laughing at everyone else. They weren't laughing anymore, and they piled on the gargoyle with fists swinging.

When Humph checked over his shoulder for Harry he had to do a double take before he confirmed that Harry was gone. He stood up to his full height—what little there was of it—searching for the playboy in the surging crowd. *There!* Harry was almost to the back door, but had run afoul of a bloodied Were. The Were was partially wolfed-out, and was backing Harry up to the wall. Humph gave up all pretense of sneaking through the crowd, running and dodging toward Harry. A cop got in his way, swinging a haymaker at Humph's jaw. He ducked the swing, spun the cop with the momentum of it, and then rabbit punched him for his trouble before shoving him away. A few steps later a mook with a switchblade tried to take a stab at him; Humph caught the palooka's wrist under his armpit, then used his free hand to break the man's elbow upward. As the mook was screaming,

Humph worked his arm over his shoulder and then threw him backwards; from the sound of it, he didn't land comfortably. Another few steps and Humph came up short to avoid a rolling furball of Weres, cops and customers both. Then he was at the back door; the bloodied Were had Harry pinned to the wall by his throat, getting ready to disembowel him with his other paw. Harry's eyes were bugged out and his face was red; he spotted Humph, though, and flailed his arms frantically for him to help.

"Hey, sunshine." The Were turned his head just in time to catch a jab augmented with silver knuckles to his brow. The Were went down instantly, his lights turned out; Harry went down with him in a messy pile, gasping for breath as the Were's grip loosened. Humph gathered Harry up, grabbing the doorknob for the back exit. "Almost there, Harry. Let's get out of here." The Boggart flung the door open.

The hallway was filled with cops, all of whom looked decidedly annoyed.

Happy cackled, and without missing a beat said, "And, behind door number three: an asswhooping!"

Humph slammed the door, then looked to Harry. "We can't go through there." Almost immediately he heard the cops on the other side pounding on the door, ignoring Happy's muffled objections. Humph searched frantically for someplace to run to; there wasn't anywhere. The front door was still plugged by cops; even if he donned a new face with his glamour, they'd be able to recognize Harry. Happy's door started splintering behind him. *Out of time.* He grabbed Harry and started dragging him toward the bandstand; it was closer than the bar, and was as good of a place as any at the moment. They were halfway there when they heard the back door finally come down.

"There he is!"

"Shoot him! Get him now!"

The gunfire was extraordinarily loud in the confines of the club. A few patrons and even cops went down from the fusillade; Humph threw Harry and then dove behind the meager cover of the bandstand. Everyone else except for the most blood-crazed and diehard of the club patrons hit the deck as well. *This is it. No way out; can't shoot our way out, and once they get us it won't be too long before they hand us over to the goons. Or maybe they won't bother, and will just put two in the back of my head while I'm "resisting" or "escaping."* He could hide in his watch, but only if he somehow managed to pass it off to someone else or hide it, since the cops would no doubt be sweeping the entire club for any evidence.

Harry was whimpering next to him. "Sorry, kid. We're out of cards to play this hand." *To hell with it.* He grabbed the top slide of the revolver, pulling it back and cocking the cylinder and hammer; going down swinging was better than buying the farm on his knees. He was about to vault over the edge of the bandstand and meet his fate when he heard something slam open behind him. Whirling around and bringing his revolver to bear, Humph was met with those same electric blue eyes from before. *The singer.* Her hair was done up in a simple bun, and she was out of her black beaded dress and into simple working clothes. But he was damned if she still didn't look like the stuff dreams and dark deals were made of.

"Well, come on! We don't have all day!" She grabbed at Harry's leg, and started to pull him in through the trap door she had appeared out of. Humph stuffed his pistol in his belt and helped her. As soon as they were all through, she slammed the small door shut and threw the latch. From the main club Humph could still hear the Jersey Devil screaming and the gunfire picking up. The were in a cramped and musty understage area, intersected with support beams, the lighting intermittent and harsh.

"Come on!" the singer said urgently, tugging on Humph's arm. He suppressed a sneeze and dodged around a tangled mess of old music stands, following her toward what looked in the shadows like a blank wall. Harry complied with being dragged along, happy enough to just be alive at that moment. The blank wall *wasn't*, however, just a simple wall; it was a metal door painted the same color as the concrete wall. She opened it into a service tunnel that was, if anything, less welcoming than the understage.

"Service entrance," she explained, "For the musicians and their instruments and things. Sometimes Jeanpaul has a magician in. The stage kind. That's what the trap door is for. This place was a club a long, long time before Jeanpaul got his greasy mitts on it." By that point they were all the way at the end of the tunnel, and she stopped and put her ear to the door, waving a hand at him. He supposed she wanted him to shut up, so he obeyed. *This broad has moxie, all right.*

"Sounds clear. My pod's out there, I always leave it at this entrance. It saves hassle at the back door." She shoved on the bar to open the door; it did so with a reluctant scrape of metal on concrete. Humph grabbed her by her elbow, holding her back while he scanned the street. He could see the red and blue of squad car lights playing against the buildings, but he could tell it was from around the corner.

"Looks clear."

The trio quickly made their way to the pod; Humph cut in front of the singer when they got to the driver's side door. "I'm driving, you give me directions." She looked like she wanted to protest, but decided against it after biting her bottom lip and thinking on it for a moment.

They spent the next half hour in tense silence; Humph making sure that they weren't followed as he did his best to follow the singer's initial directions and hurry without standing out in traffic. The last thing that they needed was to get pulled over. Harry was somehow managing to be quiet. Maybe the idiot had finally gotten some sense knocked into him. Circling the area the singer had directed them to, Humph realized that it was a storage facility: one of the big box ones that rented out individual units. Lots of security to keep undesirables out; the singer supplied a passcode and flashed an ID to one of the gate guards. Just like that, they were in. They parked the pod in the lot, which was mostly empty, and entered the building. A short walk, an elevator ride, and a few twists and turns brought them to the unit that she was apparently paying for.

"Inside, quick." She pressed her hand to a biometric reader and then punched in another string of characters to a keypad; the door rattled up, and the three of them shuffled inside. It was simple; a small cot, a net station, and a half-sized fridge were the only furnishings. Piled against the back wall were some crates and trunks. "Home sweet home, as they say," the singer offered with an apologetic smile.

They just stood there for a moment, everyone feeling awkward. Harry, surprisingly, was the first to talk. "Uh, shall I fix something to drink for everyone?" He went over to the fridge, opening it. "Oh, yeah, we've got some things to work with here." Humph nodded absently to him, and the singer did the same; they kept their eyes locked on each other.

"So. Are you going to tell me who you are, or am I going to have to guess?" The singer stood there with her fists on her hips, appraising the Boggart. "I'm guessing that the dust-up back there was over you and pretty boy here, judging by the way those cops were coming after you. Did Jeanpaul sell you out for money or something?"

He held up a hand. "Before we get into that, I think introductions are in order. First, I'm Humphrey."

She blinked. "You're a Boggart. Humphrey B—"

"Yeah, yeah. I'm a private investigator. The sap behind me is Harry Somerfield; son of my latest client. I was hired to find him. That's where this whole can of worms got opened up."

She gave him a quizzical look. "But if you were hired to find him, why was everyone after you?"

"Exactly the right question to ask. Some sort of frame up is what I think; they're saying I kidnapped him. Had to deal with some goons when I found him, and they were clearly looking to snuff him." He sat down, sighing. "What about you? What's your name, and why did you help us?"

"My name's Lori." It was her turn to look embarrassed.

"Lori the Lorelei—"

"Hey, don't blame me, I went for most of my life without a name!" She flushed angrily. "It's not my fault the first human to snare me had no imagination whatsoever!"

Humph chuckled. "I feel your pain, darling. Still, why did you help us out? I'm guessing that you were free and clear of the club pretty soon after the ruckus started."

Her flush deepened. "It was the imp. I mean, it was the spell the imp used. I mean—it's a long story."

Humph looked around; Harry pushed drinks into both of their hands. "I think we've got time." He took a long draught from his; it was a rather good martini. He suspected that Harry had quite a bit of experience making his own drinks, from whenever he'd been kicked out of whatever establishment he'd worn out his welcome in on any given day. "The beginning is usually the best place to start from."

"The rat bastard that snared me sold me to Jeanpaul. I might have been able to escape from the wretched human, but Jeanpaul…" she shuddered. She took a sip of her martini before continuing. "Whatever you *think* you know about him, I can tell you that you are probably only scratching the surface. Anyway he bound me to him—and as nearly as I can tell it was only so he would always have a singer for that club of his. He loves that place more than anything or anyone."

"That's your answer as to why Jeanpaul sold us out; someone got to him, threatened the club if he didn't turn us over." He motioned with his drink for her to keep going.

"So one night, I bailed out an imp who was short the cash to pay his tab. I felt sorry for the little guy, and he's from the same part of Old Earth as I am, but more than that, I was pretty sure that an imp would be able to get around

Jeanpaul's binding and break me free. He was drunk—or maybe desperate enough—to agree. He *was* about to face the wrath of Alphonse, after all." She sighed. "But what I forgot was that an imp can't ever do anything in a straight-forward manner."

Humph had dealt with imps before; they were wily as hell, and horrible at parties. "What's the twist? How'd the mischievous little bastard sucker you?"

"After he worked the magic and I freed him from his obligation, he told me that the binding wouldn't actually *break* until I met someone who would bring more trouble into my life than I'd already had. At that point, I didn't care; I just wanted out from under Jeanpaul's thumb. But nothing happened for *weeks*. I figured that the little rotter had conned me. Then *you* walked into the bar." She gave him another full stare with those luminous blue eyes, and Humph got another jolt. "See what I mean?"

It was everything he could do to keep from stroking her face right then and telling her that everything was going to be all right. He fought down the urge and finished his martini to brace himself. "Well, darling, I hate to say it, but the imp did one over on you. Big time. Trouble does not even begin to describe what I brought with me. I'm in a world of hurt right now, and I don't rightly know who put me there. Or why, for that matter." His jaw tightened, and he ground his teeth unconsciously. "But I'm going to figure it out."

Harry sat down between the two of them, grinning and holding his own martini. "Don't worry, miss. With my intrepid companion here, we're sure to figure this out in no time." He leaned in closer, shouldering Humph out of the way slightly. "So, where back on Old Earth are you from again, doll?"

She sighed, and tried to lean to see around him to Humph. "Germany is what you'd call it. Anyways—"

"Ah, *fraulein!* How in the world did you ever come to be on this miserable little rock?" He leaned in her way again, sipping his martini.

"It's complicated," she said as she tried to look to Humph again. He had leaned back at this point, watching the show unfold to its inevitable conclusion, which he had already guessed. "So—"

"Come now, it can't be that bad, can it? Tell me your life story, beautiful, and I'll give you the world." Harry had turned the charm up all the way at this point. Humph felt like warning him for half a second, and then decided he'd enjoy just watching the train wreck more.

Lori looked him straight in the eye. "Fine. I used to use my voice and my powers to lure men to horrible, tortured deaths on craggy rocks, and I enjoyed doing it too, until a sorcerer captured me, then sold me to a voodoo priest who bound me to his soul. Satisfied?" Harry looked at her closely, saw that she wasn't making a joke, gulped, finished his drink in one slug, and then stood up.

"I, um…I think I need a refresher. Anyone else?"

Humph was chuckling to himself. "I'm fine." He leaned forward again, smiling. "Got that out of your system, princess? He'll just be at it again once his goldfish memory resets, y'know."

"They never learn," she sighed. "What's our next move? My plan was to hop a freighter off of this rock to parts unknown; anywhere that Jeanpaul wouldn't be able to find me."

But Humph shook his head at that. "Can't leave the planet, not anymore. For starters, the bulls will no doubt already have every station monitored, and all the spaceports. If they're not running interdiction on all outgoing transports, I'd be very surprised. Jeanpaul, the rat bastard, might've had the resources to sneak us out, but he's obviously not an option anymore. Secondly, this is where the mess started. If I'm going to figure out how to get clear of it, it'll be here that I find the information I'm lookin' for."

"I don't imagine that we can sit in this storage unit forever." She glanced over at Harry. "The booze will run out soon enough, and then I might actually kill that poor sucker."

He had to chuckle at that. This was certainly his kind of woman. "Fair enough. First thing we need is a little breathing room; this part of town has become mighty crowded, fast." He sat thinking for a few moments, taking another sip of his drink. "We're going to need you to work a little of your magic, Lori. And we're going to have to skip town. Are you up for that?"

She chewed her lip, then raised her glass. "As we used to say in the old days, in for a penny, in for a pound. We're stuck together now."

And, predictably, a little more liquid courage had given Harry back his aplomb, or at least, his chutzpah. "Any man would like being stuck to you, gorgeous," he leered. "Want to try it out for size?"

"Sure. I need something unimpressive to mount on my wall." She leered back. "Are you volunteering? Darling?"

It took some convincing to get Harry and Lori to go along with it, but Humph had come up with a semi-workable plan. Lori, being the only one out of all of them that didn't yet have her face plastered on every wanted notice on the planet, would be their "front man" for the time being. First order of business was to get outfitted, literally. She went out and bought them some new clothes. Harry's suit was tatters at that point, and Humph needed something besides coveralls and a trenchcoat. Some button-down shirts, nice slacks, and comfortable shoes for both of them; nice enough to swim between middle and upper class in a pinch, but not so expensive that they stood out. Lori had a small wardrobe already, but got herself a few dresses, tops, and other necessities anyways.

The next part required a bit of subterfuge. Humph knew they wouldn't be able to get off-planet; if the cops hadn't already been watching for them to escape that way, which was unlikely, they certainly would be now. Jeanpaul had probably divulged everything about their meeting to the cops or whoever had gotten to him. *There'll be a settling of accounts on that one, Paulie. Bet your bones, you rotten fink.* Still, he could use that to his advantage. He and Lori started trolling the bars near the spaceport until they found one particularly disreputable establishment; it didn't seem to have a name, only a sign that said "Cantina" above the door. After spending some time studying the crowd, Humph found their marks; a scruffy looking freighter captain and his Yeti copilot. Lori worked her magic on both of them, and soon they were ready to eat out of her palm. No one else in the bar seemed to notice, or care. She probably wasn't the first of her kind to come a-hunting around here, and for the most part, the Sirens, the Loreleis, and the other mesmerizing types did tend to stick to fleecing their targets rather than killing them outright. Any sufficiently talented Norm hooker could do *that* sort of "magic"—the fleecing, that is, not the killing.

Using a script that Humph had made her memorize, she convinced the captain and his copilot that she was in need of help, and that they were her only hope. First she convinced them that they needed to take her and a couple of friends to a port on the other side of the planet; she was fleeing a jealous ex-boyfriend, and couldn't use regular transportation. Second, that they needed to spin a yarn for any cops that they happened to come across after they left the Hub; that they had taken on passengers, a Boggart and a human that fit Humph and Harry's descriptions, and dropped them at a random station. Hopefully that would keep the authorities chasing their tails, and off of Humph's scent. Her magic worked perfectly on the inebriated pair; they were already enamored with her before she started, and the magic itself would last for days. Plenty of time for the Boggart, Harry, and Lori to be far away when it wore off.

Gathering up Harry and their meager possessions, they were off with the captain. The flight was short, only about four hours. The primary advantage was that in-atmosphere flights didn't have to be registered the same way as launches off-planet were; no paper trail to link back to where the trio were heading. Humph dozed for most of it, while Lori was left to fend off the advances of Harry and the Yeti; occasionally Humph would wake up long enough to caution Harry against pissing off the copilot too much. Yetis weren't exactly known for their gentle dispositions. Lori actually seemed more amused by the situation than anything. This might have been the first time in a long time that she'd been at liberty to tell someone *no*. Humph didn't like to think what else that Jeanpaul had had her doing besides singing. Because if he thought about it too much, he'd have to put Jeanpaul on the top of his personal Bucket List. *In Paulie's case, meaning the short list of people I beat to death with a bucket full of cement, starting at the feet and working my way up. And if he ain't just a tall bastard.*

Once they had landed and concluded a tearful farewell—Humph had never seen a Yeti cry before; it was, in a word, disturbing—the trio set off to find a place to start plotting their next move. The port was more of the same as the rest of the planet, but grimier. To put things into perspective, Jeanpaul's establishment had rested on the periphery of a zone like this, slightly on the higher end. This area had everything together, jam packed and stacked on top of itself. Factories and power plants were nestled right next to pleasure districts and gunshops, with casinos and churches just around the corner. The ports were the real face of Planet Mildred, and this was the perfect place for them to disappear into for awhile.

Humph picked an out-of-the-way flophouse; he had Lori pay in advance for a one-week rental room. A few extra bills slipped to the clerk was pretty much required; places like this one housed those on the lam as often as they did transients and factory workers. Only she and Harry walked in; Harry's face was buried in bags that he was carrying for Lori. Humph, meanwhile, rode along via his pocket watch, which he had temporarily entrusted to the siren. When they were finally settled in the cramped room, Humph started to get to work. Using a cheap, disposable comm unit he started to put feelers out to some of his more trusted contacts. He needed more information on Harry's company, Somerfield Botanicals, the various subsidiaries and other connected businesses. He also needed to know if anyone was making big moves in order to find Harry; someone with a lot of resources was after him, and that sort of influence was hard to hide effectively.

The only thing left to do was wait. He had sent out the messages as securely as he could; unfortunately, he wasn't as good at cyber security as Fred. It would take a bit of time for any responses to come back. This left a lot of time to kill in the flophouse room. Harry kept hitting on Lori. Humph had to give him some credit for persistence. Lori continued to shoot Harry down, but each setback seemed to embolden him rather than dissuade him. That didn't really surprise Humph; he doubted that the word "no" was something that Harry had heard very often in his privileged existence.

What did surprise him, however, was when Lori started making passes at *him*.

Subtle passes. Probably so subtle Harry didn't even notice them, and thought *he* was free and clear to navigate. Then again, courtship among Paras tended to have little nuances involving magic that Norms wouldn't see.

Like the little tendrils that looked like golden dust that Lori kept throwing off in his direction. Or the distinctly *magical* gleam in her eyes when she glanced at him. And the undertones of her voice when she spoke to him—undertones that told him, in essence, "I could use my power on you if I chose, but I choose not to, so you know this is real and not a compulsion." All this read "I am really, *really* interested in hooking up with you" in Para language. This was dangerous. Paras and Norms loved...differently. Paras experienced wild changes in emotion that could only be described as hyper-bi-polar, running to deep longings and passion that could burn deep in a being's heart for millennia. After all, in the old days it might be a hundred years before you encountered a potential mate. Or longer. You'd better be able to hold to affection for at least that long.

There were several other problems with this courtship, of course. How much of this was actually due to the imp's spell? He had no idea. Another consideration was Harry. While Harry wasn't exactly high on Humph's list of all-time favorite people, pissing the Norm off and having him stomp out of the room—possibly to blow their cover before Humph could reel him back in—was a pretty bad idea. While it was clearly not going to happen between Harry and Lori, Harry didn't know that.

And then there was Claire...dear Claire. Parked in the back of his head, smirking at him, and reminding him that he still wasn't "over" her, no matter what he might think. He never "fell" for anyone; it was a rule of his, or it had been. Especially a Norm; he was going to be around for awhile, whereas most Norms just...weren't. Those were the breaks. Claire was different, and he was still kicking himself for letting her in. Thirty years had never seemed like such a long time until after he met her. Granted, she had turned into a colossal bitch, and a Fang bitch at that. He knew, however, that he was at least partly responsible for who and what she had become; a mixture of pity and heartache always cropped up when he started thinking about her.

And Lori is a Para, not a Norm, a little voice in his mind reminded him. She was dangerous, certainly. A killer of men; Humph had never heard of a Lorelei who wasn't; she had spent hundreds of years doing it, before she was bound. It was her nature. *But you're no different, Boggart. What have you done in your long life? For survival, for kicks, for money?* He was really starting to hate the hell out of that little voice in his mind.

They were sitting in the room, sharing drinks with the vidscreen droning in the background. Humph had been keeping an eye on it for any little bit of intel that he could glean. Most media outlets were in the pockets of any number of interested parties, but gems of information could still get out every now and again. Then *it* happened.

"So. How long have you been—" Lori gestured vaguely in a way to suggest "the world" "—out of the broom closet?" She blinked limpid blue eyes at him. "It hasn't been more than a couple of years for me. I never would have thought anyone would have gone looking for one of my kind up that particular obscure Austrian stream. I'd thought I was pretty safe."

Humph mused thoughtfully. "It's been a while." He left it at that, not wanting to tip his hand too much. "Let's just say it was a surprise to the both of us when I got yanked out into the Norm world."

Lori made a face full of distaste. "If I ever get my hands on the bastard who wrote *Summoning and Binding for Dummies...*" Her expression made it clear that what she had in mind was going to be long, involved, and painful.

He raised his glass. "Not so bad, being out in the world, though. They have scotch, after all." Humph drained his glass. "Beats a share of a farmer's crops, at any rate."

"And your farmer didn't brew his own?" She smiled sweetly. "Really, Boggart, you should have found a better class of host."

Humph shook his head. "I never said I was a particularly good Boggart, lady." There was a moment of comfortable silence, and he felt *it* again; the urge to throw caution to the wind and go after her. He had to give himself a hard mental shake. It was an effort to stand up and walk over to the bottle on the bed instead of throwing his arms around her.

Harry was still passed out on the bed, empty martini glass in his hand. *Nice that someone is able to sleep, at least.*

But when he got up, so did Lori. Before he could turn, she was behind him, close enough so that he could feel her warm breath on the back of his neck. "So...since Sleeping Ugly is going to be out cold for a while, think we could go somewhere else more...comfortable...for a little?" Her voice was a warm, lush purr in his ear; she didn't physically touch him, but he could feel tendrils of her magic twining seductively with his. "I'm sure we could manage something."

Keep it together, Boggart. "Can't do that, sweetheart. This poor sap is my—our—lifeline right now. I'm not letting him out of my sight for more than a minute at a time if I can help it." He stared at his drink for a second, taking a large gulp to steel his resolve. "I might not be a good Boggart, but I like to think I'm at least a passable gumshoe." He could smell the light perfume that she was wearing; it was blue lotus, and was intoxicating on its own. His head was swimming when he finally turned around to face her. Electric blue eyes locked with his; he wanted to tear himself away from her, to sit down and pass the time quietly, but he found that he couldn't.

"Oh, Boggie," she breathed, moving in a little closer. "He's finished off most of that bottle of gin. He won't be going anywhere for a good long while. Why don't we get to know each other better?" She was almost nose-to-nose with him. "A whole...lot...better?"

His hands started to move of their own volition. He set down his drink, then gently took the back of her neck into the other hand. It felt like time was stopping, and that he was going to fall into her eyes and be lost forever. Their lips were almost touching, uneven and hot breath gracing one another. It was like a scene from *Beauty and the Beast*; he was savage and feral, she was frail and innocent. He closed his eyes, ready to surrender to the inevitable. Everything shattered when his comm unit went off loudly and insistently.

Harry bolted upright in bed, still half asleep. "—no, not on the carpet!" He blinked hard a few times, looked around, then remembered where he was. "Uh, the phone's ringing." Humph and Lori quickly stepped back from each other; Humph felt guilty, and he could see the disappointment on Lori's face. *Too damned close, moron. You* know *better.* Harry was oblivious to the exchange.

Humph picked up the comm unit. It didn't take very long at all for him to see that things were going downhill fast, and picking up speed. Over the course of the next couple of hours, Humph had bad news piled on top of worse news. Most of the contacts that he had reached out to never got back to him. The Harvey Brothers, Mikhail, Rodney the Fence, Small Tony, Big Tony, Señor Leandro, and Whispering Miguel; all of them were silent, and quite a few of them were his most dependable information brokers and snitches. Everyone he did hear from didn't know anything of value. What stood out was that they were all scared. Which was saying something, considering the clout some of them had and the strings that some of them could pull. There was someone out there making big moves, and all of it seemed centered on Humph.

The last of them was Lenny the Lip, who sounded on the edge of a nervous breakdown before the Boggart closed the connection. He sat down on the bed heavily, feeling weary. He had been in the dark on jobs before when a lot was on the line, but this was different. Someone had painted a bull's-eye on his back, and he didn't like it one bit.

Well, this wasn't anything that someone who was merely holding a grudge against the Boggart could pull off. It was one thing to have an APB out on him for kidnapping someone who wasn't quite kidnapped. It was quite another to put out word that he was toxic that reached all the way down to every level—and have it believed enough that his sources wouldn't even touch base to say they knew nothing. *Or it could be worse than that; maybe some of them didn't call back because they couldn't; mighty hard to pick up your phone when you're dead.*

"We've got big trouble, dollface," he ruminated, as Lori watched him with a gaze that had gone from seductive to worried as each call came in. "This is either big corporate, or big crime. Or both, sometimes it's hard to tell them apart. That's people that can spend more than you and I will see in a hundred years on five minutes of organizing." His eyes turned to Harry. "In fact, it's probably more than his mommy's company will ever see in a hundred years, and *that* just doesn't add up. I can't figure how you'd be worth the cost and trouble for all of this. No offense."

Harry spread his hands and grinned magnanimously before taking another sip of his refreshed martini.

Humph's comm unit chirped again. *More bad news.* It was an unlisted line. Most of his contacts—even the legitimate ones—made use of burner comm units with reusable lines; that way *he* would know who it was, but it'd be a lot harder for anyone that was paying attention to find out who was calling. He picked it up after a few beeps. "Hello?"

"Hi there, Boggie. I'm going to screw your head off and play golf with your spine for all the trouble you've caused me, you know."

Humph blinked hard as recognition set in. "Claire?" Relief washed over him; she had been in the back of his mind ever since he got the first returned call, and the implications of someone not getting back to him had become clear. To be honest…no matter how his *head* felt about her, down in the emotions sector, he'd been worried sick about her. Sure, she was pretty well protected by her hive on that station of hers…but it wasn't that hard for a Norm hit squad to take out a Fang. Especially the kind that had the sort of money that allowed you to build an entry-pod, hide it in the bay of a freighter, pop out when you were docked, go straight to the section of the station you wanted to hit, cut an entry port and dump the squad right in the target's office.

"Yes, it's me, you bastard. What have you done this time?" Humph caught Lori's expression; whatever she was reading in his face, she was *not* happy about it. In fact, *her* expression looked a lot like jealousy.

"Not much. Shot a bunch of goons, saved a blue-blood playboy from getting a permanent haircut at the shoulder range, and I've been accused of kidnapping the same."

"Ha fucking ha. Really, what did you do?"

He explained the situation to her from the beginning; the job from Bevins, the hotel, his partners going missing and his office being ransacked, and being on the run. Claire took a few seconds to process everything once he was done. "That doesn't make sense."

"You're telling me, sister. Only thing I can figure it for is a rival corporation or some big shot criminal enterprise. Problem is, I can't finger anyone who would fit the bill."

"It can't be either one of those. Boggie, *I'm* on the god-damned lam."

It was his turn to be stunned. "*What?*" Claire had serious backing, probably more than any other person that he knew. Her operation had grown in the few years since he'd last seen her; the Elders were grooming her for proper leadership, since she was bringing in *real* money now with all of her ventures. The Elder Fangs pulled a lot of weight; plans and schemes and machinations that stretched into the century range to see the result, information networks that rivaled those of governments, and more money than God. *Could they be behind this?* The implications made his stomach lurch hard a few degrees to port. It didn't seem likely; he didn't know if he felt that way because of the scarcity of evidence of if it was because he simply didn't want to believe that this whole mess was that far-reaching.

"I got your message a few days ago. I put it off since I was busy. A pesky business rival needed some re-education; a girl has to have her hobbies, after all. Anyways, once I got back to my station, I started digging into your little problem from what scant information you provided me. A few hours later, everything went straight into Hell's own crapper; we lost our communications, my accounts were frozen, and then the station was attacked! I barely made it out in one piece; as far as I know, no one else did. I've been on the dodge ever since."

"Holy hell, Claire. If I had known—"

"Damn right if you had known! Whatever fucking trouble you're in, I'm in now too. I'm telling you, Boggie, I don't want any part of it! At first I thought it was one of the other Clans making a move; it wasn't. This was different, at least outwardly; whoever is doing this is well trained, well funded, and going after anyone and anything with a connection to *you*. They're burning all of your bridges and trying to run you to ground, Boggie."

His mind was swimming with all of this new information, trying to process it. "Look, Claire, tell me where you are. We can figure this out—"

"Stop right there. I'm on the run, and I'm staying that way until this is over, Boggie. I'm not going to be the grist for the mill in this goddamned escapade of yours. I took a big enough chance just calling you, and I only did that to see if you knew anything that could help me. Fat lot of good it did me. Whatever shit you got yourself into, you can get yourself out of. Good luck." With that she closed the connection. And if she was smart—which she was—she ditched the comm she'd just made the call with somewhere in deep space, before course-correcting for a tangential trajectory. He wasn't sure, but he thought that he had heard just a trace of concern. He could have just as well been imagining it.

Well. That was...festive. "Huh." So Claire was on the run; whoever was after him was making sure that he had no one to turn to and nowhere safe to hide. This was beginning to look and feel a lot bigger than he thought even five minutes ago. But who could have the juice to pull all of this off, and stay in the shadows while they were doing it?

"Well?" Lori was sitting on the bed next to Harry now, her arms crossed in front of her chest and her expression icy. "What did *she* have to say?"

"That someone shut down and attacked her station right after she started poking at our anthill. She's a Fang Hive Mistress and until a few hours ago she owned a deep-space station. So you tell *me* what that means." Humph hadn't intended to be quite so point-blank—except that if Lori was going to get all pissy over another woman, that needed to be burnt off at the root, right now. They didn't have any time for that sort of thing; this was a survival situation. "Harry, do you have any idea who could pull all of this off? It can't be your mother or the company, can it?"

Harry shook his head, his brow screwed up in concentration. "I really can't, Humph. We're just a cosmetics company; we've got our rivals, sure, but no one who would have the sort of scratch to go to these lengths to just rub me out." He rubbed the back of his neck, then grinned. "I mean, I am pretty awesome when you get down to it, but it's not like I'm vital to the company or anything. Bumping me off wouldn't hurt things with our board; hell, some of our investors might even throw a party. Especially ol' what's her name…never did forgive me for that trip to Mars with her daughter…" He snorted. "And never would believe me when I said it was Brittany's idea."

Lori stood up; her arms were still crossed defensively across her chest, but at least she didn't look like someone had just kicked her dog. Actually she looked scared. "Paulie never let slip who had leaned on him; he didn't really share much information with the hired help. I can't really think of who it would be myself; I'm not exactly an experienced member of the criminal underground, after all." She looked back and forth between Harry and Humph. "Well? What do we do now?"

There was a very loud bang from the front of the flophouse, where the check-in desk was. They were all startled by the sound, but Humph immediately knew what it was. *Breaching charges. How could they have found us, again?* Scratch that. *How could they have found us so soon?* He immediately set to work, gathering up the essentials, kicking Harry in the ass, and pushing both Harry and Lori toward the door. There were more explosions; flashbangs, then gunshots. Whoever was raiding this place, they weren't interested in taking prisoners. The rest of the residents of the flophouse had the same idea as Humph and company: Get the hell out of Dodge. The hallway was packed with screaming beings, Para and Norm alike. Humph was in the rear, with Harry between him and Lori. Everyone was tripping over each other, stampeding toward the back door. Humph and his crew were by no means the only ones with reasons to run from the law in this joint.

After a lot of noise, elbows, and stepped-on toes, they were out the back door and into the cool night air with the first lot of escapees from the flophouse to fight their way into the open. They didn't so much stumble out as tumble out, barely managing to stay upright. Humph had taken the precaution of keeping them a little back, so they didn't run straight into the arms of whatever dragnet had been set up outside all of the exits. Floodlights came on within seconds of them emerging from the building, blinding everyone. The gunfire started almost immediately after, cutting down the first rank of people in front of them. Humph shoved Lori and Harry hard to the right, diving after them. He felt something akin to a heavy punch hit his left side, followed by searing pain. They all landed in a pile, behind what looked like a burnt-out transport. Everyone from the flophouse was still piling out, being pushed from behind by the raid team right into the gunfire. There was a lot of screaming; the hot, thick scent of blood that wasn't his hit his nose. Right on top of that was the burned-pork reek of lethal laser-wounds. It was a slaughter. No warning, no demand for surrender or quarter given; this was a sweeper team, and they were going to kill everyone that they saw. They might not even be human. Bots were not supposed to be armed, ever, but everyone knew that, just as Asimov's Third Law was an old joke, anyone with enough money could shrug off the fine if he was found with a garage full of war bots.

"We're pinned down," Humph gasped out. The pain was working its way up his side; he glanced down and saw that he was definitely bleeding freely. It was a gunshot, not a laser blast; if he had been tagged by a laser, there'd be less blood and a hell of a lot more pain. At least there was that; no major organs had been hit either, but he was still going to have problems if they didn't get out of here and stop the bleeding soon. He probed the wound, felt the pocket torn through, and panic shot through him; his pocket watch was *gone*. It must've been shot away. If he couldn't find it, he was dead. As a Boggart, he was tied to it; he couldn't go too far away from it, otherwise he'd be instantly transported back to it. He felt himself getting dizzy; he staunched his wound with his hand, mumbling about his watch and needing to punch a way out. Lori shouted something to Harry; all sound except the screams of the dying and the gunfire was starting to fade out.

Things were going dark around the edges of his vision; Humph knew he was going to pass out soon. Lori had disappeared. Had she left them? Had she ever been with them in the first place? Harry was shouting something, trying to keep him awake. Then his face swam in front of Humph's vision; Harry was smiling, flashing his perfect teeth. How could he be smiling? How *dare* the little punk smile? Harry patted Humph on the shoulder, and then *ran* into the kill zone. He jumped over bodies, bullets kicking up flecks of concrete and dust all around his feet, impacting all of the surfaces around him as he made his mad dash. He stopped right in the center of everything; there were still a couple dozen people scrambling to find cover before being cut down. Harry calmly bent down, picked something off the ground, and then ran back to where Humph was propped up against the burnt vehicle. The bastard was still smiling.

"Hey, you dropped this, partner." Humph stared at him incredulously for a few seconds before he looked at what Harry was holding up: Humph's pocket watch, smeared with a little bit of blood but otherwise intact. "Every man needs to keep a good watch." Humph blinked for a few seconds, took the watch, pocketed it, and then promptly passed out.

The Boggart woke up in stages. At first he could only register pain; it wasn't sharp and immediate like before, but dull and throbbing, distant. Next there were sounds; he eventually recognized them as voices, Harry and Lori's. *Everyone made it out. How? Where are we?* The last was his vision; he had passed out a few more times before he finally came to fully. He recognized the ceiling; the interior of a modular transport ship. Hundreds of thousands of them were mass produced every year, to the same specs by different manufacturers.

His first thought was to panic, since if they were off-planet they had just posted a huge red arrow pointing right at themselves. No way they could have gotten on board a ship without someone IDing them. And every ship leaving this system *was* being searched, that much he was sure of this late in the game. Anyone who could afford a strike team that could take out a Fang Station could afford damn near anything, up to and including buying off the planetary police. And after all, he *was* wanted for kidnapping. It would be a small stretch for him to be "killed in the course of re-sisting arrest," or some other convenient fiction.

Something was off...the ship didn't have any power; there was no hum from the atmospherics, no lighting other than a cheap hand torch turned into a lamp; he recognized one of Lori's scarves draped over the top of it, diffusing the illumination. He looked around, and soon realized they weren't in space; the large, gaping hole covered with a tarp at the aft of the ship was a pretty big indicator. Harry was close by, sitting on an empty storage crate. "Hey, you're awake!"

"Where?" Humph tried to speak more, but the single word was the only thing he could croak out; he was dehydrated, at least partially from all the blood loss.

"Lori found it. Old spaceship graveyard. We dragged you here, and she started to patch you up a little." He pointed down to Humph's side; there was a crude, but clean, bandage over his wound. "She'll be back soon; once she is, it's my turn to try and find some stuff to hold us over here." Harry shook his head. "You should have seen her, partner. When we were pinned down back in town, she didn't run out on us. She just slinked up to a couple of the goons—you know how she can *strut*—and whispered something to them. They put down their guns, just like that! Then she—" He stopped short, shuddering. "Well, she picked up a piece of glass, and just like, opened their throats. Both of them were smiling when she did it, too. Creeped me out a little bit, I'll tell you."

Humph coughed. "Kid, she's a Lorelei. That's what they *do*. Lure in men, cut their throats. We're damn lucky she happens to want our throats intact." He wasn't sure if the warning was going to take—the kid was as sharp as a bowling ball sometimes—but he would have felt guilty if he didn't at least try.

There were footsteps outside. Lori swept the tarp aside, standing in the ragged entrance. "Well, look who lived through the day. Hiya, handsome." Harry was about to start speaking, thinking she was talking to him, but stopped himself short with a sheepish chuckle when he realized she was addressing the Boggart.

"Hiya yourself. Looks like I owe both of you; I'm not terribly comfortable with that." He was feeling a little bit better; Lori or Harry must've given him pain meds at some point when they were stitching him up.

"Get us out of this mess with our skins intact, and I think we'll be able to call it even." She stepped into the shuttle, walking over and handing him a bottle of water. "Got a few things from a guard shack at the entrance of this dump. It's not much; Harry's going to need to go out soon to see if there's something he can pick up. Figured it would be better to rotate who goes out, limit our exposure that way."

Belatedly, Humph remembered the handful of prepaid credit chips he'd taken from Harry. Grunting with effort, he reached into his pocket to see if they were still there.

They were. Blood-crusted, but intact. He started to chuckle. Because "blood-crusted" would have raised another enormous red arrow if he'd been *human,* and his DNA was on file like every other human. The law mandating that DNA be on permanent file went all the way back to the 21st century. But he wasn't, and given that having a portion of a magic being's blood meant you could control said being, there were even laws making sure no one ever got the chance to put what passed for their DNA on file. Part of the weekly "housekeeping" chores the Boggart did for himself and the agency was to run a cybermagical routine making *certain* if anyone had gotten a speck of blood, their data was well and truly scrambled. Harry could pass those cards with impunity, and no DNA-sniffer would get a whiff of the Boggart.

"Here," he croaked. "Wash 'em off. Lori, rough the kid up a little so he looks like he belongs around here. Harry, think you can act like a drunk? Not a sloppy drunk, just a little happy."

Harry grinned. "I think I can manage it; I've been practicing for most of my adult life."

He thought for a moment. "Then there's bound to be liquor stores all over this part of town. Find the ones with food. Buy booze and grab food as if it's an afterthought, like the wife sent you out for some and you're taking the chance to get yourself another bottle. Don't buy too much at any one place. When I say too much, I mean, you buy the cheapest, smallest bottle, and maybe 20 creds worth of sundries over that. Got me?"

"Got it!" Lori broke out a compact of makeup, then proceeded to get Harry in character. Smudges of grease, dirt, and a few applications of her stock of beauty products got him looking the part: disreputable and cheap. Harry finished the disguise with the proper swagger of someone with a decent buzz on. Once he was gone, Lori took up a seat on the makeshift bed.

"How're you feeling?" She laid a hand tenderly on his arm. He propped himself up with some effort; the pain in his side ramped up a little, but he was able to bite it back.

"I'll live. Thanks again, by the way. Let's not make it a habit, you saving my rear." This was an uncomfortable position for him to be in, in a lot of ways. Usually when it came to women, he was the one doing the saving. Or at least, when there was saving needing to be done, Claire notwithstanding. And now he owed Lori. He didn't like owing anyone anything. He'd gotten where he was by amassing unspecified-favors-to-be-paid-later, not by being in the position of having to pay one out. Then there was Lori herself. A Lorelei. A species not known for their warm hearts. How much of this supposed attraction she had for him was acting, how much was due to the geas, and how much was real?

"I know it's probably ironic of me to ask this, but I don't suppose you happen to have any more water in that sack?" He chuckled weakly. "You being a Water creature and all that."

"First thing I thought of, since you were going to be dehydrated." She got up...and every movement of every inch of her was seductive as she walked away from him...fished another bottle out of the sack, and swayed her way back. "I also found where there's a clean tap; I can refill these so don't go all manly on me and crush them."

They sat quietly for a few minutes as he sipped at the water. Lori watched him the entire time, and Humph did his best to avoid her gaze, occupying himself with his thoughts. Lori was the first one to break the silence.

"We shouldn't be here," she said. "I don't mean *here* here. I mean messed up with these damn humans."

"It's kind of their galaxy now, darlin'. We're just living in it."

She sniffed. "Oh yes. *They're* the 'normals.' We're the ones that—aren't. Humans always have been trouble right from the time they started to put thoughts together in their little ape-brains. And they can't see anything without wanting to use it, own it, exploit it, or run over the top of it. Look what they've done to you and me! We were minding our own business, never causing any trouble, and then—*bam*. Geased. Used. Enslaved."

"You're going to learn to get over it sometime, kid. Shit happens, then you deal with it." He sighed. "I've been out in the world a lot longer than you have, so maybe it's just that. But you can't hold onto that kind of hate; there's no money in it, for starters. Besides, it's not like our kind is exactly blameless in the annals of history; there's a reason that Norms have stories about the boogeyman, boggarts, and even little siren *frauleins*. That reason isn't particularly cheery. If you're preaching revolution, you've got the wrong boggart."

Suddenly, and without warning, he missed his partners. If Skinny Jim and Fred had been here…he'd have had not one, but two foils to fend off Lori. He'd have had someone to keep an eye on Harry at all times. Skinny Jim didn't even sleep; he'd have had someone he could trust to stand watch while everyone else did.

He'd gone decades without having partners; he'd always been convinced he didn't need them, didn't need *anyone,* and now look. A handful of months with those two lugs cluttering up the office and he felt crippled by their absence. *Is this what it's like for Norms?*

And where were they? Were they even still alive? Or—at least, what passed for alive in Jim's case? He'd always been told that Paras who worked together for a long time or had some sort of bond could at least tell when something Bad and Permanent had happened to each other, but he'd never been in the position to find out. Mostly he had put that down to an old wives' tale; more than a few Paras got caught up in their own bullshit and myths. Now he hoped that it wasn't. Still, it was better if Jim and Fred were in the wind or taking dirt naps than in the clutches of whoever the hell was after him, that much he was certain of.

Lori pressed on, undaunted. "Fine, fine. I'll put away the placards and slogans. But more immediately...shouldn't we ditch Harry? If we didn't have to worry about him, we could disappear, lose ourselves out there. We've got enough money to get by, at least for awhile." She laid a hand on his arm. "We could run away together, Humph."

The Boggart stared into her eyes for several long moments, searching for how to answer. "The thought has crossed my mind, more than once. The kid is a stone around our necks sometimes; he just doesn't know how to walk on our side of the tracks." He paused before continuing; he thought he had heard something outside, but quickly dismissed it. "Despite that, he's been starting to pull his weight. If he hadn't managed to snag my watch back at the flophouse, you'd be short one boggart. Even though he'd more than likely be toast without me, he still stuck his neck out in a way that not a lot of beings would've for an old P.I."

"So that's it?" he could tell that Lori knew she was defeated, but still harbored some hope that he would change his mind.

"It is." He had to be firm with her, to stamp this notion out once and for all. "The kid is all right, despite being a spoilt nincompoop. We need him as much as he needs us, if we're going to get to the bottom of this and come out of it alive. Besides, even if we did ditch him, we're in it too deep now; whoever is after us will keep coming after us until we're dead. That's what my gut says on this one; whenever I start going against my gut feelings is when shit goes sideways on me."

She let out her breath in a long hiss that reminded him that some people claimed the Sirens and Loreleis were somehow serpentine in nature. "I never got involved in anything this twisted before," she admitted, finally. "My kind are pretty straightforward: If we like you, we like you; if we don't, you're dead. And there wasn't a lot that Paulie wanted out of me but simple seduction; he never let me in on any of his complicated schemes. I guess I had better stop trying to ride on my own instinct and follow yours."

The Boggart relaxed. The last thing he needed right now was a recalcitrant Lorelei on his hands. She was a great asset…and she would have left a serious hole in his planning if she decided to cut her losses and leave them. "Thanks, Lori. I need you on my side to help me figure out how we're going to get out of this pickle. Now, what's taking Harry so long?"

Lori shrugged, taking a sip from his bottle of water. That sick feeling in his stomach came back. Humph debated internally, then started gathering up gear; he checked the revolver, made sure it was still fully loaded. "I'm going to head out, see if I can find what's taking Harry so long. I've got a bad feeling for some reason." That part caught her attention; concern creased her brow. "If I'm not back in three hours, take the money and disappear. No guarantees, but you might be able to slip off alone if you're careful."

"Don't count on me doing anything that sensible," she retorted. "Let's hope this time your gut is wrong." She grabbed him by the ears and kissed him, releasing him again quickly. Then she slipped off into the bowels of the old derelict; he hoped she had herself a hiding place or a back exit or something down there in the darkness. He didn't waste any more time; he started off out of the hole in the craft, his pace quickening as he oriented himself in the ship graveyard. He broke into a full-on sprint when he heard a commotion on the edge of the lot; it was near one of the entrances, between the lot and an adjoining street. Humph stopped short of the exit, quickly catching his breath and steadying himself before he carefully peered around the corner of the wreck he was hiding behind. He drank in the details immediately; Harry, shouting obscenities, and being manhandled by two hired guns in suits into an all-black and tagless transport before having a black bag roughly pulled over his head. The suits followed him in, slamming the doors shut after them. But the vehicle did not immediately speed off. Maybe they figured there hadn't been anyone watching them. Or maybe they needed to secure Harry a bit more before they moved.

I've got to move fast; if they take off and get into traffic, I'll never be able to find them again. Humph put on one of his standby disguise faces; he made sure it was one of the ones he hadn't used in quite a while, just to be safe. He quickly ran a few dozen yards along the fence and away from the transport before he found a hole in the enclosure big enough for him to slip through. *Shit! It's taking off!* The transport was just starting to lift off the ground, readying to join the air traffic. Humph looked around frantically, then ran out into the street to stop a passing aircar; he was almost run over for his trouble twice before one, a junker that looked like it was on its last legs, stopped for him. The driver was a Norm male, and was less than happy with the Boggart. "Fuckin' idiot! Tryin' to get yourself kill—" Humph had gone around to the driver's side, punched the man in the jaw, and ripped him out of the vehicle before he could finish his sentence or properly react. He slammed the door and scanned for the transport. *There!* It had already lifted off and was moving to merge with traffic; luckily, this wasn't his first time performing a tail, and he knew all the tricks. Tails were a lot easier—and safer—with multiple vehicles, but he didn't need any with this bunch; they didn't seem at all concerned that someone might be following them. Still, he played it cautious; the last thing he needed was to tip his hand and turn this into a proper chase.

Or worse, end up with them chasing *him*. Whatever happened, he needed to get Harry back, alive. Thoughts raced through his mind as he followed the transport: *Did Lori feed Harry to the wolves, tip off the goons to get rid of him? Would she do that to save her own neck? Is she doing that to me now, that final kiss to seal my fate?* Loreleis…they were all about themselves. Well, that was what he'd heard, anyway. All Paras that used fascination as a weapon were cold. He supposed it came as part of the territory; how else could you stand to lure someone in, seduce him, then off him, up close and personal, yet oh-so-impersonal?

It wasn't long until they arrived at their destination; it was a medium-sized warehouse, buried in one of the more run-down industrial sections. The transport went into landing mode and parked in front of the entrance; since the traffic wasn't as sparse in this part of town, Humph flew past, then turned a corner a block down before parking himself.

"This could get messy," he muttered. He hated going in cold, not knowing the strength of the opposition, the layout of the building, or any of the other numerous little details that could kill or save him. But this time the Boggart didn't have any choice; checking and readying his revolver one final time, he started walking toward the warehouse. His destination was the rear door, maybe loading docks if the place had them; with any luck, the security there wouldn't be as heavy as the front door. His single best hope was that Harry's captors had no idea there was still any opposition left.

He rounded the corner, then found his way next to a trashcan fire that was burning unattended. Humph pretended to warm his hands as he studied the rear of the building; it didn't appear that there was any external security. No cameras, sensors, or guards, at least that he could make out. *Maybe they had to set this place up in a hurry. Or maybe they're not planning on sticking around all that long. Either way, I need to get in there and get out with Harry, the sooner the better.* He made his way slowly over to the warehouse door, crossing the street and trying to look like just another bum down on his luck, stopping to peek inside dumpsters and trash cans—at least, the ones that weren't on fire. Once he reached the door, he did a very quick check on it; not even so much as an alarm appeared to be hooked up to it, just a simple lock. It took him a few minutes of working at the lock with his picks, but he finally cracked it. Slowly, he opened the door, then slipped inside, closing it behind him. He had just enough time to place the picks back into his pocket with his watch when he heard a voice from behind.

"Put your hands up and turn around slowly, or you're a dead man."

Shit. Humph grabbed his watch, then complied with the demands, raising his hands and turning around slowly. He was greeted with the muzzle of a rather mean-looking shock-gun being held by a rather mean-looking guard. One squeeze of the firing stud, and the Boggart would either be incapacitated or fried to a crisp.

"Please, mister, I was just hungry an' lookin' for food! Don't kill me!" He whispered urgently, then proffered his watch. "Here, take this! It's the only thing of value I have, I swear!" He dropped the watch, then kicked it with his boot so that it slid behind the guard."

"Shut up, and keep your hands where I can see them." The guard reached for his radio, then blinked hard; the trespasser had disappeared before his eyes. He didn't feel a thing when Humph clubbed him over the back of the head with the butt of his revolver. Humph caught the man as he slumped to the floor, setting him down gently. He checked for a pulse; there was none. *That's the thing about getting hit in the head; if it's hard enough to knock you out for any significant amount of time, it's also probably hard enough to damn near kill you. Tough break.* Humph had a quick burst of inspiration. He started to strip the man down, putting on his uniform; a simple black jumpsuit and a load-bearing vest with tactical gear. To complete the look, he changed his face to that of the guard's, scooping up his shock-gun.

"Thanks," Humph said as he wedged the dead guard's body between a couple of shipping crates; hopefully no one would be able to easily stumble upon him there. There was something incredibly pathetic about the whole little scene; one poor idiot, dead in his underwear, crammed into a space full of dust and mouse turds. Helluva way to end your life.

Shit, he probably deserved it. No time to ponder it now. He did his level best to act casual; he needed to put off the vibe that he belonged here, after all. It took him less than a minute to get to the center of the room through the labyrinth of shipping containers. Humph didn't like what he saw; there was a cleared space in the middle of the room, with Harry tied to a chair with the black hood still over his head. There were two suits standing in front of him, arms crossed in front of their chests and smug grins on their lips. Three more guards were spread out in the open space, all of them with shock-guns; probably more elsewhere in the warehouse. Harry was saying something, but Humph couldn't make it out, so he walked closer.

"...you bastards just wait! You're going to regret the day you ever, *ever* laid a hand on me. My mother is going to make your lives hell!"

The suit on the right casually leaned forward and slapped Harry through the hood, hard. "Whatever you say, pretty boy. Just wait until the boss gets here; then we'll see how much you feel like issuing threats that your ass can't cash." The suit checked his watch, then chuckled. "In fact, he ought to be here in just a couple of minutes."

There were too many guards for Humph to fry before he'd get fried in return; they weren't grouped close enough together to get all of them in one blast, at least without hitting Harry in the process. He had to come up with something fast; whoever this boss was that the suit was talking about, Humph was pretty sure he wouldn't be alone when he arrived. He kept walking closer, then found what he was looking for. Keeping his shock-gun ready but trying to be discreet, he strolled up to a control panel and started to quickly punch in commands. The suit that had slapped Harry took notice.

"Hey! Simmons, you're supposed to be patrolling your sector of the perimeter. What do you think you're doing?"

"Redecorating." Humph mashed a final button. Machinery whirred to life overhead as a crane activated with a hum, swinging down and then flailing crazily. It struck a stack of containers, sending them toppling over; the topmost one crushed one of the guards as the others scattered. The suit looked back to Humph, disbelief being replaced by rage just before he caught a blast from the shock-gun; he burst into flame, jerking wildly with the voltage. The other suit and one of the guards managed to dive out of the way of the shot, scrambling for cover from the falling shipping containers and the shock-gun. Humph ran over to Harry, who was squirming in his seat from all the loud crashing and weapons fire. He grabbed Harry, tearing the hood off. "Hold still!"

"Don't kill me!" Harry started squirming harder.

Humph took a second, then dropped his glamour in annoyance, revealing his true face. "It's me, dumbass! Hold still so I can cut the rope!" He extended his claws, then started sawing at the rope around Harry's wrists.

"Humph? Humph! You came to save me? How'd you find me?" With a final cut, Harry's hands came free.

"Fewer questions, more running! Let's go!"

The shipping containers were still being knocked over as the crane followed the erratic and conflicting instructions Humph had programmed into it. The guards and the suit were starting to recover; Humph sent a blast from the shock-gun their way, even though they were outside of its pitifully short range; it'd give them something to think about at any rate. He grabbed Harry by the arm and then shoved him toward the exit. Both of them started running, skidding to stops and dodging as crates and containers rained down all around them. Fortunately the same falling objects were making life just as difficult for their pursuers. It was pandemonium; between running herd on Harry, dodging the falling crates, and occasionally shooting over his shoulder to dissuade their pursuers, Humph had his hands full. One guard ran into their path; Harry actually gut-punched him, shoving him out of the way before continuing his dash. At some point—Humph didn't even remember how—he picked up a second shock-gun.

The exit suddenly loomed in front of them, salvation for at least a few moments. Humph could still hear shouting and barked orders from behind them over the din. He and Harry burst through the warehouse door one after the other.

"What now? We can't lead them back to Lori!" *Kid is actually starting to use his head. If we live through this, he might actually be worth his salt.*

"Here!" Humph reached into his belt, pulled out the revolver, and thrust it into Harry's hands. "Go hide behind that dumpster on the other side of the street, I'll be right there!" Humph had to work fast; he fished out a torsion wrench from his lockpick kit and jammed it into the emitter of one of the shock-guns. Then he keyed the firing stud, using the grip from the other shock-gun to keep it depressed; the shock-gun started to emit an insistent whine that was growing in intensity with each passing second. Humph set the jerry-rigged guns down gingerly, then sprinted as hard and fast as he could over to the dumpster that Harry was hiding behind. Harry startled for a half-second before he recognized Humph. "Gimme the gun!" Harry handed the heavy revolver to the Boggart; Humph took very careful aim at the shock-guns, and waited.

Seconds later, the door to the warehouse burst open. The remaining suit and at least two of the surviving guards were there, guns at the ready. Humph couldn't help but grin as he fired the revolver; the Webley-Fosbery was an old, accurate gun, and it struck true. The bullet hit the power pack of the jammed shock-gun, breaching it; both guns exploded brilliantly. The blast was enough to momentarily blind Humph and knock him onto his ass. When he was able to right himself, he and Harry peered over the edge of the dumpster at the same time. Where the suit, guards, and door used to be was now only a ragged, smoldering hole the size of an aircar.

"How the hell did you do that?" Harry's jaw hung open in awe of the impromptu destruction. "I mean, finding me and then the thing with the crane and blowing up the guns?"

Humph shrugged, helping Harry to his feet as he stood up. "Just winged it, kid. It ain't exactly my first rodeo. C'mon, we need to get out of here before the 'boss' shows up." They hoofed it to where Humph's stolen aircar was still waiting; there was some fresh graffiti on it, a quick one-color tag of what looked like a gang-sign, but otherwise it looked undisturbed. Once they were in the air, Humph made sure not to beeline straight back to the ship graveyard; still, they had to hurry. The clock was ticking and if Lori actually did what she was supposed to, she'd be in the wind in the next half an hour. He had some questions for her, if his suspicions had any merit.

"Why'd you come after me?" Harry had a look on his face like a puppy that had been caught rummaging in the garbage.

"What are you talking about?" Humph asked, annoyed. "Why wouldn't I?"

"Well...I overheard you and Lori. Talking about ditching me and running off. I figured that you didn't want me around anymore; she sure doesn't." He looked down at the floorboards. "So I made a call, or tried to. Those guys in the suits grabbed me right after, and you know the rest."

Humph couldn't take his hands off the controls to smack himself—or Harry—in the head, but at that moment, he dearly wanted to. "Aw good Christ, kid..." he groaned. "Look, I tried to explain. Lemme try it again, this time you're sober, maybe you'll get it. Three things. One: You're stuck with me, I'm stuck with you, because whatever is going on around here, it's gonna take both of us to figure out enough to get these bastards off us. Whoever they are, they're huge. Whatever it is you somehow got yourself into, *it's* huge. *They killed an entire Fang space station just to keep us from getting help.* But that means somehow, something we know or can figure out is dangerous to them. You got that part?"

Slowly, Harry nodded.

"OK. Two: Lori is a Lorelei. At best, they're cold bitches, and she has a real hard case against Norms. Don't worry about her; it's better if neither of us is involved with her, anyways. That dame is trouble with a capital 't'; if anything's true, that most certainly is."

"Yeah, I suppose. What's the last thing?"

"The last thing is we haven't been paid yet. And the job ain't done till the Boggart gets paid. Right, partner?" Humph turned to give Harry the full-on toothy grin, Boggart style.

Harry returned the grin, his spirits evidently lifted. "You got it, partner."

The pair arrived back at the ship graveyard after taking a circuitous route; Humph was a lot more careful than the goons that had nabbed Harry, and was continually checking to make sure that they weren't being followed. They ditched the stolen aircar and the guard's uniform several blocks away and continued on foot, just to be sure. Finally they made it back to the ship they had set up sanctuary in; Humph could see light very faintly past the edges of the tarp. When they were less than half a dozen paces away, Lori stepped out. She instantly looked alarmed.

"Stop!"

It was too late; before either of them could react, the ground gave way under Harry's feet; flailing around, he hooked Humph's collar, dragging the Boggart down after him. They both landed in a very uncomfortable pile at the bottom of the hole. *At least there aren't any spikes. Or saw blades. Or snakes. Or all of the above.*

"Ow," Humph croaked out. The hole was about six feet deep, and hastily dug; the corners had been squared, though, so whoever had dug the trap at least knew what they were doing.

"You're sitting on my chest and you weigh a ton!" Harry was somewhere underneath him; it took them a few moments to untangle their arms and legs, stand up, and dust off.

"Lori, you mind telling me what the hell is going on?" Humph was in no mood for this nonsense; they didn't have time to be screwing around, since the goons could show back up here and take them all out in short order. He looked up; Lori was peering over the edge of the hole. Then her face was joined by two more; one rather desiccated, the other slowly changing from fur-covered to average Norm-looking. "Sonofabitch."

"Really, the first thing you can think to say to me after all of this is a dog joke? You're losing your touch, boss." Fred was scratching his chin as the last of the fur receded, his face now back to its usual unremarkable self.

"Well, we've always known I had the brains in this operation. Get it? Huh, get it?" Skinny Jim had the "helmet" from his bot suit under one arm, elbowing Fred with the other.

"If you two jokers are done, I'd very much like to get out of this hole. Today. Right now."

"It's the boss, all right. Bitch, bitch, bitch," Skinny Jim quipped, reaching down and throwing Humph the end of a rope. "I swear, here we are, turning up, protecting his fair damsel, fortifying the castle, and all he can think is to complain."

Humph hauled himself out, and offered Harry a hand to help him scramble up the dirt wall. "Glad to see you idiots," he said gruffly. "Dammit, I thought you might have gotten fragged when I couldn't raise you."

"Aww, see now? He cares!" Skinny Jim clapped the bot head back on. "You weren't nearly as hard to keep track of, boss. Whoever is behind this really didn't give a rat's ass about us, you and pretty boy there were who they wanted. All we had to do is get to Fred's hideout, and sit tight, and watch the news."

Fred nodded solemnly. "Once we saw where all the shit was going down, we knew you had to be in the middle of it. We got the general loc, then I sniffed you out. Took awhile; the ol' nose is a bit off after a century of smelling deadheads. Anyways, tracked you here from the flophouse where all the killing got done. Water Wench here gave us the rundown, then told us you'd gone after the kid, so we hunkered down to wait."

"I've got one other question." Humph looked back to see Harry climbing out of the pit. "Why dig the hole?"

Both of them shrugged. "We were bored, and it seemed like the thing to do." Jim hooked a thumb back at Fred. "Besides, someone had to bury their treats." There was a light clang as Fred slapped the back of Jim's helmet.

"Well, can't argue with that. Next time, don't let me fall in it."

"What, you don't like looking up to us?"

Fred snickered. "He's already short enough for that, Jim."

"I wonder if a dog and a real robot would be any less annoying than you two. Probably make less of a mess."

"But they wouldn't dig holes nearly as good."

Harry joined the circle, still dusting himself off. "Harry Somerfield, I present to you the rest of Boggart, Barkes, and Bot; Fred and Skinny Jim, respectively." After the introductions and handshaking—Harry was somewhat reluctant to shake hands with a Reboot at first—were over, Humph instructed everyone to gather up what little there was in the shuttle; they had to get out of the area and find a new place to hunker down and plot their next move.

"Way ahead of ya, boss. But, I'll warn you," Jim said. "It's not the Ritz."

"More like the 'fritz,'" Fred admitted.

"What's that supposed to mean?" Humph asked, raising an eyebrow.

"You'll see when you get there."

It looked like a World War II bunker. Literally. Superficially, at least, it didn't look as if there was a single piece of modern tech in it—or at least, hadn't been brought in by someone else. Right now, the light was being supplied by portable lamps. Living conditions were pretty basic. Six metal-frame bunk beds bolted to the floor had been made up with surgical precision, and Humph was damn sure the linens were some form of military surplus. They just had that look to them. There was a kitchen area with a stove that apparently ran on fuel cells; a couple of metal tables were also bolted to the floor. There was a bathroom at one of the far ends with an incinerating toilet and a water-recycling shower. The bunker looked as if someone had welded spaceship hull-plates together into a pair of square tubes, put the thing together in the form of an X, and buried the whole thing. Most of it was taken up with storage; food in the form of concentrates, water, other supplies.

"The hell," said Humph, once he'd climbed down the ladder and surveyed the place. "How in the name of all things dark and dangerous did you find this place?"

"Bought it," Fred said. "For cash; Furs never trust Norms. This is a standard bug-out bunker you can pick up on the black market virtually everywhere there's a planet. Well, we don't call 'em bug-out bunkers, we call 'em emergency dens. We make sure they're off the grid and off the radar. Some Furs even go so far as to hand-dig their dens, or put 'em in cave systems." He pointed to a single thin wire running up the wall, and from there, up the access tube with its ladder that led to what looked like a standard city utility hatch.

"That's our sole connection to the outside. I found a planetary data-node and wired into it. Otherwise, we could bolt the hatch and not come out for a year if we didn't feel like it. That's how Furs can go missing for years, decades at a time."

Humph whistled. "I like how you think," he said.

Lori dropped down onto one of the bunks. "It's more comfortable than it looks!" she said, with a look of surprise.

"Standard ship mattresses. We figure on hibernating if we have to go under. Saves consumables." Fred went over to the stove and fired it up, emptying a couple of pouches into a pot and adding water. "You don't want to hibernate on a bad mattress."

"I don't suppose—" Lori began.

Fred nodded toward the storage. "One-size-fits-most T-shirts and pants. Hot water in the shower module."

Lori got up quickly and headed for the storage crates. Clean clothing clutched to her chest, she edged past them and disappeared into the bathroom. Humph sniffed appreciatively. Maybe the stuff in that pan was also some form of military ration, but after the last several days, it smelled like a gourmet dream.

Lori came back out some time later, hair wet and bound up on the top of her head, face innocent of makeup, just as the food was ready. Fred divided it equally among all of them except for Jim, who waved at the bowls and said "I ate already." Humph wasn't going to argue or inquire as to *how* Jim had eaten; instead he dug into whatever-it-was—some sort of casserole—and damn near licked the bowl clean. He noticed that neither Lori nor Harry were any more fastidious than he was about doing the same. They hadn't gone hungry, but the adrenaline had rendered them all famished. Fred passed around coffee, or what passed for coffee, when they were all about halfway through.

"Short story," Fred said, collecting the bowls and stacking them in the little sink. "We got about two minutes' warning before all hell broke loose on the office. And that was only because they cut off all our comm just before they hit. We used the emergency exit, headed for one of the safe-houses, discovered it wasn't so safe after all, and I declared FUBAR and hauled Jim here. All we did was monitor what was going on after that. Sorry, Boss, but the best thing we could do was not to go after you, but to disappear. We needed to drop completely out of sight first and let them figure we'd bailed on you."

Humph nodded. This couldn't have been Skinny Jim's plan, but it made perfect sense for Fred. The Fangs had reverted to their old medieval arrogance after the Great Uncloseting, but the Furs, it seemed, had retained a lot of their old paranoia. Good thing they had.

"That's where I started tracking you," Skinny Jim said. "I bet it isn't going to shock you in the least to hear that most of the people after you aren't law enforcement."

Lori had already curled up on a bottom bunk, but wasn't looking sleepy. Humph stayed where he was, in the metal chair. It wasn't comfortable, but he wanted to keep a little distance between himself and the Lorelei. "I was beginning to think along those lines, yeah," he admitted.

Harry had hoisted himself up into a top bunk, and was watching them all like a superfan following the ball at a tennis match.

"If anything, the law was reacting to what was going on *after* the fact," Jim continued, pulling his bot-head off and putting it on the table. "Take the raid on Jeanpaul's place. That wasn't cops. The cops only showed up *after* the shooting started. Radio chatter started and they were *pissed*, then suddenly the radio chatter stopped dead, and the only thing that came over the freqs was an order to withdraw."

Humph nodded. That fit in with a growing suspicion in his mind. He turned to Harry. "OK, kid," he said, gruffly. "Spill me some beans. Who'd you call when you bugged out on us and those goons grabbed you?"

"My mother," Harry said, sheepishly. "Or—actually, the head of Company Security." He frowned then, thinking. "Or, actually, I *tried*. It was the right number, but I didn't recognize the voice of the person I talked to. He cut me off and told me to stay put, and it wasn't more than a minute later that those thugs turned up and—"

"And I saw the rest." Humph cut him off. He patted his jacket, then retrieved a cigar, the last one in his case.

"Not down here, boss; don't want to tax the ventilation system any more than we have to."

He shook his head. "Naw, I'm not going to smoke it, just chew the hell out of it while I think. This entire mess has more twists and turns than a Medusa on a bad hair day."

"Well," Jim said, after a very long pause. "Elephant in the room. I can't think of any multi-planetary business that can push local law enforcement around the way we've been seeing. I very much doubt even the Mafias or Tongs could do it. So, that leaves us with—?" Jim had learned to signal a lot with his voice alone, since what was left of his face didn't have hardly any expression to speak of.

"What, Feds?" Fred shook his head. "How does that make sense? We're not exactly all that high on anyone's wanted list, at least before this fiasco started. Whoever these goons are, they seem to want Harry, but for what? He's just a rich kid with too little sense." He held up his hands. "No offense."

"None taken," Harry replied.

"Anyways, we're all small-time in the grand scheme of things. And even if it were the Feds, which ones? Planetary? Earth-gov? One of the alliances out on the rim?"

"Fred, you and me, we watched a lot of old vids and movies. I *know* Humph has. When it isn't *who* you are that's dangerous, it's what you know." Jim tapped his metal-encased finger on Harry's head for emphasis. "And that's doubly true when you don't know what you know. When you were in the right place at the wrong time, for instance."

Humph stopped chewing on his cigar to speak. "I've been thinking on that. I don't think it's anything that any of *us* know; we've dug up stuff for all sorts, and hell knows that we've trudged through enough crap to maybe get a whiff of something we shouldn't have. But it's nothing earth-shattering; if it was, we'd have been able to suss it out by now." He looked at everyone in the group before settling on Harry. "Which leaves just one person that this could be about, though it doesn't make much sense."

Harry put up his hands in frustration. "We've been over that, though. I *really* don't know anything, nothing that could bring this kind of trouble."

There was silence for a few moments. Humph jabbed his stogie in the direction of Jim. "While you two have been off the radar, have you been keeping at the digging I told you to do for this gig before it blew up in our faces?"

"That's a 10-4 chief," Jim replied. "Incentive and boredom, don'cha know. Harry has been a very naughty boy, haven't you, Harry?"

"Well, yeah. I already told Humph about all of that, though. Sure, I was embezzling, but that's small potatoes, right?"

"That alone isn't enough to draw down this kind of thunder, that's for sure. There's something else to it, though."

"When is a raven like a writing desk?" Fred said, suddenly, as if something struck him out of the blue.

"I have not been smoking the Caterpillar's hookah, nor eating and drinking things that say *Eat Me* and *Drink Me*," Lori put in, crossly. "And my name isn't Alice."

"The point of that riddle, because it was nonsense, was to make children try and figure out a way that a raven *could* be like a writing desk," Fred explained. "Turn the reasoning around. We're sitting here assuming that there was nothing Harry could possibly have gotten into to bring this kind of attention down on him. Turn it around. Assume there *must* have been something he did, and start looking for it from the back end."

Humph turned in his seat, looking to Fred and Jim. "Did anything stick out to you two when you were digging around Harry's misadventures in economics?"

"Why did you pick Nightshade Ltd. to plunder?" Jim asked Harry.

The playboy shrugged. "Same reason I picked all of the others: It was small, isolated from the rest of the company, not really involved in most of our day-to-day activities. I figured that no one would notice if some money went missing; just shuffle it all around to make it disappear. Hell, if the banks can do it, I could, too." He frowned. "Why do you ask?"

"Because if I were an auditor, I'd be pulling in the CFO and everyone in the chain down for interviews right now," Jim said with authority. "I could tell what was you—you're crude and unsophisticated, and you left fingerprints all over what you stole. It's the five or six *other* people in there that I'd be worrying about. For a little company it's drawing outside resources all out of proportion to its size, and they aren't coming from the main firm, either. Then those resources disappear. I found not two sets of books, but *four.* There's property on one of those sets of books that doesn't appear on the public books, or any of the other two sets. That property is eating a lot of utilities, and I mean a *lot,* the kind of power-draw that used to signal someone was running a drug greenhouse. That ringing a bell?"

Humph felt his jaw dropping. He had taken Skinny Jim's word for it when the Zombie had claimed he'd been a bookkeeper for the mob in life…he'd had no idea that the Reboot had been *that* kind of bookkeeper. This was Fed-level forensic accounting! "That sounds like a lead to me. Right now we don't have any other moves to play; we don't have enough to go public and expect to live, and getting off-planet isn't exactly the safest bet either. Whoever is doing this has reach."

Lori sat up from the bed, alert. "What're you thinking of doing, Humph?"

"I'm tired of being on the defensive, always running from whoever these bastards are. I think it's time to take the fight to them, to get proactive." He stood up, replacing his cigar and chewing on it as he talked. "I say we raid the damned place that Jim found, see what we can see."

There wasn't a lot of privacy in the bunker, but Skinny Jim and Fred had either gotten a lot more sensitive to Humph's body language or they'd figured out something was going on between Humph and the Lorelei some other way. In either case, they both pulled Harry into an intense interrogation about Nightshade Ltd. around the kitchen table, giving Humph a chance to get down into the end of one of the storage arms on the excuse of looking for some firepower.

"No need to sneak around, Lori. I know you're there." He turned around to find her standing at the entrance of the storage arm, hand against the frame. Even in a generic shirt and trousers, she still looked enticing.

"You're not going to let me come with you, are you?" she said, although the way she said it, it was more like a statement than a question.

"You're right, I'm not." Humph crossed his arms in front of his chest, readying himself; he knew that this wasn't going to be an easy conversation. "You've been a trooper so far, Lori; you've saved my hide, and that's something I don't take lightly. So I'm going to save yours; you need to get clear of this while you still can. We're going to be causing a lot more trouble, and that means we'll have more trouble heading our way, likely. That ought to give you a better shot of getting safe, while they focus on us."

"What if I don't want to get safe?" she countered. "I know Loreleis don't have the best reputation in the world, Boggart, but we're not all bad. I never killed anyone I didn't have to. If we get out of this, I could be a lot of help to you—"

"You already said the key word, darlin'; 'if' we get out of this. We're all way out of our league on this thing; getting by on dumb luck—especially in Harry's case—and dirty tricks are the only reasons we've all stayed in one piece so far. I don't imagine that our lucky streak is going to last much longer, especially since we're probably about to poke the tiger with a stick."

She moved closer. "So? Shouldn't you use everything and everyone you've got? I just found you, Boggart. I don't want to lose you. I don't let many people get close to me, much less this close."

The Boggart could already see the tendrils of her magic seeking him out, trying to caress him. "People who get that close to me don't have the best track record, Lori. I've left enough bodies in my wake; I really don't need another person I'm close to added to that number."

"It's not just your decision, Boggart. It's mine, too." She had him penned in the end of the tunnel now. It was obvious that she wasn't going to just sit back and take what he planned. Not without an argument...maybe a fight.

"Damned if it is your decision!" He angrily took a step forward, but Lori held her ground. "I'm not going to let you throw your life away trying to help us."

"Let? *Let?* I was making my own decisions thousands of years ago, Boggart! What makes you think I'm going to sit still and let you treat me like you're a caveman with his hand wrapped in my hair?" She blocked his way with her hands on her hips. "Admit it, Boggart! You're just afraid—afraid of *me.* Afraid that if you admit you have feelings for me, every bit of your control over things is going to go flying out the window!"

"All right! I am afraid of that! I do care about you, you silly little girl. A helluva lot." He was fuming, and had to take a breath to calm himself. "I'm afraid with you around when this gets worse than it already is, I won't be thinking clearly. I'll be too worried about you, wondering if you're safe. And I need every bit of attention for what's to come; if I don't have it, we're all dead even surer than we probably already are." He took a final step forward, leaving less than a foot between them as he took her by the arms. "If I know you're safe, away from this, maybe, just *maybe* we'll get out of it. Probably not, but it's still a shot." Being this close to her was maddening; her magic was mingling with his, and he could feel her breath against his neck and chest as he looked into her eyes.

She looked up into his face, and for once, he didn't see a single trace of guile about her. "This isn't the geas, Boggie. I know what it feels like to be manipulated by magic. You're the first man in a thousand years to get to me. I don't want to lose that."

"Then do this one thing for me, Lori. Get out of here, run, hide and be safe. I won't be much good to you if I'm dead."

"And how do I find you again?" she asked, her eyes filling with tears.

She wanted comfort and that was the one thing he couldn't give her. He never made promises, even implied promises, that he couldn't keep. "We'll just have to see, kid-do." He kissed her; softly at first, then more urgently. And, of course, the kiss was interrupted by a polite cough from the other part of the bunker.

"Boss, if we're going to make a run, we need to decide if it's now or later. And if it's now, we need to plan." Fred's voice echoed from far enough away that it was obvious he wasn't within eyeshot of them…

…now. No telling if he'd gotten a full view of the clinch. *I don't know whether to kick the tar out of that fleabag or buy him a case of scotch for interrupting.* Humph and Lori separated; she was still wiping tears from her eyes and trying to smile.

"If I could shoot…or turn invisible…or pick locks…" she said, her voice thick with tears.

"I'd still want you to run, to find someplace safe. This is just how it has to be, Lori." He caressed her cheek, then thought better of it and let his hand fall away with some reluctance. "Get together the cash we have left over on the cards. Jim ought to be able to arrange something for you while Fred and I are on this little mission." He chuckled lightly, looking down at his feet. "I imagine that you can take care of yourself pretty well, if anything comes up. You're a survivor."

Before he could say anything else that he might regret, he pushed her gently aside and called out to Fred. "Now. They don't know we know about Nightshade. And they don't know you two hooked up with us. We hit them while we still have some pretense at surprise." It took every bit of his resolve but he edged past Lori and back to the main module.

The first thing they needed was a vehicle. Amazingly, there were half a dozen in the ship graveyard that only needed a couple of parts to get running. Some quick can-nibalization by Fred and they had another beater-transport, virtually invisible. Some clever get-arounds by Jim and they even renewed one of the tags, so they wouldn't even be stopped, registering the thing to the graveyard. It would be a nice little present to their involuntary hosts if they all survived this.

Now it was the Boggart and Fred in the transport, and a single burner phone. Lori, Harry and Jim were hunkered down in the bunker with only the data-node hack running. The Boggart didn't know what their plans were if everything went to hell, and he didn't *want* to know. *Makes for less that someone can beat out of us later.* He just hoped that Lori was gone by the time he got back; he didn't want to have to go through another emotional goodbye. Twice in one century was over his limit already.

Nightshade Ltd. was housed in a neat, antiseptically clean research park, full of little companies just like it, all in identical white buildings finished with a shiny ceramcoat— which alone would tell the knowledgeable that what was going on here was something biochem or tech in nature. If something went terribly wrong, the building could be tented, fumed, and hosed down. With or without victims still inside.

And that was…interesting. Because this was supposed to be a cosmetics researcher. So…why put it in a BioHazard 4-rated park?

"What do you think we're going to find in there, boss?" Fred had been uncharacteristically fidgety on their ride over. He knew what the stakes were, and how low their chances of success were. It said a lot about him that he decided to come along despite that. Humph just hoped that his friend's loyalty wouldn't be the death of him.

"Hopefully something that'll give us an out, something to get free of this mess. If we can't get our hands on that, we're sunk."

Their plan was simple; that way, fewer things could go wrong with it. The downside was that if anything went wrong they were probably going to end up dead—or worse. They were going to sneak in as a delivery crew; coveralls, some dollies with boxes loaded with really heavy parts and things that looked like expensive machines borrowed from the yard, and the transport completed the picture. Bullshit their way in the front door, and move as fast and stealthily as they could until they found some dirt. They were sitting in the transport outside of Nightshade Ltd.; Humph took a moment to look over Fred. "Are you ready for this, partner?"

"Yeah, I'll be fine." He looked anything but fine; Humph tossed his flask into Fred's lap, grinning as he put on one of his disguise faces. This one was of a dockside bartender he had met centuries ago, back on Earth; boxed-in ears, a flat nose, and darkened eyes completed the picture: just another beaten-down laborer.

"Never leave home without it," he said, pointing to the flask. "Take a nip, and then we're on." Fred did so, downing quite a bit more than a nip of the whisky before handing the flask back to Humph. With that, both of them exited the transport and started unloading the boxes. They affected their best "worn out and ready for happy hour" expressions as they trundled up to the entrance of the building.

Long ago, firms had figured out that having a bored, minimum-wage guard on the door was actually more effective than having a sophisticated, AI-run security check-in. A few too many incidents with bots letting in people just like Fred and the Boggart, and incinerating legitimate, unexpected deliveries, had led to going retro. As advanced as bot tech was, there was still something to be said for a living element somewhere in the decision making; though Humph had heard rumors and conspiracy theories about some places experimenting with cyborgs and other gruesome inventions, fusing living beings with machines. As expected, waiting at a desk at the loading dock was a guy who looked like a tired basset hound, with the tell-tale whiff of whiskey about him, behind a little white desk with a rack of monitors on it. And old-timer like him was perfect for a gig like this; just there to collect a paycheck, too jaded and exhausted to ask too many questions other than, "When's lunch?" *Just another piece of the puzzle.*

"Delivery for Lab 3," Fred said, as the guard waved them forward. It was a gamble, guessing at their "destination," but it paid off this time. Places like this weren't usually big on creatively named rooms. The guard took a box cutter and opened Fred's container, and the exhaustion in his face was pathetic. He knew that if the delivery was for a specific lab, that lab expected it to *be* there in the morning. He also knew there was no one to get it there but him....

"Buddy, you look beat. We'll haul this shit in for you, if you want," the Boggart offered. "Us little guys gotta look out for each other."

The guard's face brightened. "Thanks, bud. I got a herniated disk, and you know those damn insurance companies, they won't do nothin' about it until I'm crippled. I get off in about five minutes, and all I wanta do is lay down."

The Boggart had been counting on that. Counting on the fact that the human guard would probably be replaced by a simple locked and warded door after hours, and counted on the fact that showing up five minutes before second shift change would guarantee them at least an hour of undisturbed snooping. Their timing was truly a piece of luck, one of the few they'd had during this entire fiasco. "Ain't that the truth. Take a load off, just point us where we need to go." The guard gave them a generalized layout of the facility; where the administrative level was, engineering, and the labs. At the end of the description, he handed them both generic-looking nametags.

"Wear these from this point on, if you don't want to get zapped. You'll see what I mean." With that, they were buzzed through the doors into the main facility. The first thing that struck both Fred and Humph was how...average the facility was. It looked like the inside of any other office building; people in cubicles, at desks in offices, and no one paying them very much mind at all. There were security cameras in all of the usual places. There wasn't any sort of oppressive, totalitarian feel to the place. It was boring. *Maybe this is how evil, Norm evil, really looks: mundane.*

All of that changed once they reached the labs. The hallway they had turned down ended abruptly with two very solid doors; they looked like blast-doors from a distance, and Humph confirmed it once they were closer. The really scary thing about the hallway were the two security bots that manned the entrance.

But the bots didn't even power up as they approached, and the doors opened silently for them. Some sort of passive scanning, probably; judging from the cannons affixed to the bots, Humph surmised that he and Fred would've been little more than scorch marks if they weren't wearing the badges that the guard had given them. The doors stood open, waiting for them to pass; the bots stood watch, still no indicator that they were even active. The hallway beyond was pristine; gleaming white on white, with the faint smell of medical antiseptic, the kind of smell that hospitals always seemed to have. They didn't see anyone for what felt like ages; just more hallways, all the exact same. Most of the doors they passed by were unmarked; several were marked "Storage," and more than a few of those were plastered with warnings about the contents.

Boggart spotted a door marked "Lab 3," and on impulse, pushed his dolly toward it. The door opened before he reached it, and Fred followed him. "What're we doing?" Fred hissed.

"I figured whatever you needed to do, you could probably do from the lab," the Boggart replied. "No? I figured outside the labs, the computers are probably kept from accessing the lab stuff, but I bet there's no such security keeping one lab from looking at another's work." He looked for a storage closet, found one, and opened the door, shoving his box inside. Chances were, no one would even look at the boxes for a week. Maybe more, given how much dust was in here and how barren the shelves were. He took Fred's dolly from him, and did the same with Fred's box. Fred was giving him a stare that said *How the hell did you figure that out?*

"I'm smarter than I look," Boggart said, and wiggled his fingers at Fred. "Make with the computer magic."

"We'll have to get into the lab proper, use one of those computers. It's going to be a closed network, otherwise we could have Jim help us out remotely. This place looks pretty secure, so no chance of a signal getting out of here, at least undetected." Fred reached into his coveralls, retrieving a data pad and a few other little gizmos; tools of the trade for the experienced hacker.

"Let's get to it; I don't imagine we'll have much time once we start messing around in the lab proper."

The pair exited the storage closet, still pushing their dollies. The lab itself was open, with various technicians working at their stations; none of them seemed to pay much attention to the two workers as they made their way around. Past some thick glass was a clean room, complete with airlock. It was a tidy little operation; a place for everything and everything in its place. Humph found what he was looking for: a terminal off to the side, obstructed by some lab equipment.

"Do your thing, furbag. Get whatever you can, and then we're out of here."

Fred immediately set to working. He plugged some of the smaller gadgets into ports on the terminal, then hooked his datapad up to it as well. Humph was keeping one eye on Fred's progress, with the other on the technicians. One thing he had noticed about this lab was that there weren't *any* cameras here. At all. That was strange, and he didn't like it one bit. It took a few minutes before he got any indication from Fred.

"Humph, this is bad."

"No kidding, we need to get moving." Some of the technicians had noticed the two of them, and were starting to stare in-between their tasks.

"No, I mean this is all bad here. I'm getting next to *nothing*."

Humph bent down, hovering over Fred's shoulder. "What the hell do you mean, nothing? We didn't get this far to leave empty-handed, damnit!" His voice was a harsh whisper; he had to keep scanning the room, as the technicians were now starting to talk among themselves.

"I mean, there's stuff here, but none of it is very useful. At least, the stuff that I can get to." He pressed a finger to the viewscreen, indicating what he was talking about. "We've got references to a lot of data, but very little concrete stuff.

'Population densities,' 'dispersal patterns,' 'delivery vectors,' 'patients,' and so on. Shipping manifests, some supply lists that I can't make much sense out of. But that's all I'm getting; everything else is behind encryption and firewalls that I'm not equipped to get past. Not even Jim could, I don't think."

"What the hell are you saying, then, Fred?"

"I'm trying to say that this is military-grade, Humph. There's no way that I'm cracking it. Hacking isn't like in the vids; for anything other than basic stuff, it can take weeks. Months even."

Military-grade? "What the hell is protection that heavy doing in a cosmetics lab?" he whispered, feeling a cold knot in his gut. "Download what you can. Grab something that looks like it needs moving and let's get out of here."

He headed for a stack of what were obviously empty boxes and shoved his dolly under them. One of the technicians was walking toward them.

"Excuse me, could I have a word with you two?"

"No need, chum, we're on our way out. Thanks, though." Fred and Humph quickly exited the lab, hoping that would be the end of it. They were what Humph thought was halfway out of that part of the facility when the announcement came:

"Security to Labs, sector 3, please."

"That's our cue, exit stage right." Humph cursed under his breath. Then he looked around. "Wait, where is our exit?"

Fred looked over to Humph. "I thought you knew the way out."

"Goddamnit, we're lost." He searched for a sign, anything. "Screw it, we've got to keep moving. If I say run, don't hesitate; just hoof it." They started quick walking down the nearest hallway; it was maddening trying to find the way out, since all of the hallways looked nearly identical. Finally they turned down one hallway that was different from the rest; through a different set of security doors, it was interspaced with clear walls every ten feet or so. "We'll use this as a reference point if we have to. Let's keep going—" Humph noticed that Fred had stopped in front of one of the clear walls. "Fred, what's going on…" He regretted the question a moment later when he saw what was on the other side of the wall. He abandoned the dolly to walk over beside Fred.

"These aren't rooms…they're *cages*." Fred's voice was low, and taking on a low, bestial rumble more and more with every word he spoke. Inside the cages there were dozens of Weres, some caught in mid-transition; every kind of Were, from bears to the big cats, though mostly wolves. And all of them were recently dead, and horribly so. Splotchy skin, fur gone in huge patches, red lesions, and too much blood spread around were the common features. Some looked like they had torn their own throats out. The entire scene was awful, and almost caused Humph's gorge to rise. "It's all the cleaner and antiseptic; I couldn't smell 'em. Weres can always tell when our dead are around…"

"Fred…we've got to go." He gently placed a hand on the werewolf's shoulder; Fred spun on him, fury and tears masking his eyes.

"Whoever did this…these bastards have to pay for this."

Humph shook his head slowly. "Now's not the time. We need to survive if we're going to make sense of this, make it right. Okay?" Fred didn't answer him; his eyes were back on all the dead Weres. Humph grabbed him by the arm. "We're *leaving*." Fred jerked his arm away, then started down the hallway at a trot. Humph sighed, then started running after his partner to catch up.

He had the sinking feeling that Fred was not listening to him; that the Fur had an agenda of his own at this point, and he wasn't going to listen to anything. Still, they were able to avoid security; they had passed a few bewildered technicians in lab coats, but no one else. Humph mentally cursed when he realized that he had left the dolly behind. Things started to look slightly more familiar as they progressed;

Humph recognized a smudge on one of the storage doors they passed. "We're getting close, Fred. Once we get to the front, act natural—hey!"

Fred veered off down a corridor, one that actually had a little sign with an arrow on it. *Engineering and Maintenance.* Now...that could be a good way to get out, since most Maintenance areas almost always have their own doors. But Humph had the feeling that getting out wasn't on Fred's mind right now.

Humph was fast, but Fred was faster; there wasn't any way he could compete with the Were's supernatural speed. Humph almost lost him a few times, and had to guess at several intersections about which way to take. He reached a terminus for a hallway, two service doors that were still swinging from Fred's passage. Humph pushed through the doors. "Fred, we don't have time for this shit! Whatever security this place has is going to be coming down on us any second—what the hell are you doing?"

Fred was at a control console, typing so fast his hands were a blur. "Thought so. Standard Home Service's Security protocol. I can frack this up in my sleep." Fred finished at the console, then began pulling levers, flipping switches, and performing all sorts of other seemingly arcane actions at different panels and control stations. Red warning lights flashed and alarms went off, then went dead and silenced. "That bought us some time." Fred extended his claws on one hand, using them to puncture the tops of several barrels before kicking them over. He then retrieved a lighter from his pocket, flicking it on after several tries. He carefully set the lighter on the ground, then turned to Humph. "We should run, before the fumes reach the flame."

"What've you done?" Humph was staring at the scene in front of him, uncomprehending.

"No time, I'll tell you on the way!" Now it was his turn to drag Humph away. They were through the doors and less than a dozen paces down the hallway when they heard a muffled *whumph*, followed by what Humph judged to be the sound of a moderately sized explosion. He chanced a look over his shoulder to see flames spilling out of the room they had just been in.

"Mind explaining before I twist your head off of your shoulders?"

"Futzed the climate control, fire suppression systems, and a few other key systems. The actual labs are locked down, but that won't save them; that little fire I started back there is going to spread unimpeded through the ventilation. Probably a lot of toxic fumes, too. That means they won't be able to put the fire out themselves and the fire services will be called. They'll never be able to cover it all up once you get three or four fire companies and a swath of reporters showing up." He smiled, looking over to Humph as they jogged. "I used to be an engineer, y'know."

"You're goddamned crazy, Fred! Ever think that your little stunt might get us killed in the course of things?"

"No worries, boss. We're almost home-free." They turned a corner to find the blast doors; beyond was the less-secure section of the building, and the exit. Humph sighed in relief, shaking his head.

Any sense of a breather ended once they were through the doors; two out-of-breath security guards, younger and better equipped than the old-timer at the loading dock desk, were there to greet them.

Everyone was still for half a heartbeat. Fred was the first to start talking. "Thank god you two are here! There are a couple of maniacs loose in the building!" He was walking toward them, arms spread wide. Humph followed his lead. *If we can get close enough, we can take them out before they have a chance to—*

Both guards went for their weapons simultaneously.

—do that. Fred was closer, and rushed forward to grab the first guard in a bear hug, pinning the guard's arms to his sides and preventing him from raising his gun. Humph

kicked the second guard's pistol out of his hand just as he was about to turn it on Fred. The guard reacted instantly, switching his attention to the more immediate threat. He flicked out a collapsible baton, readying himself. Humph moved forward, extending his claws; he had to stay inside of guard's swing, otherwise he'd be sporting broken bones at best. And these guys obviously knew how to handle Paras. The guard was good; he backed up, swinging in tight arcs to keep Humph from getting too close. Humph caught Fred and the other guard still struggling from the corner of his eye; they had rolled forward into the hallway, and the guard was trying to get on top of Fred and pin his arms to the floor with his knees. Humph made a split-second decision, turned and kicked at the guard Fred was fighting; he flinched away at the last second, causing the kick to take him in the shoulder instead of his temple.

That gave the second guard the opportunity he'd been looking for; he lunged, bringing the baton down on Humph's left forearm. Luckily, it was a glancing blow since the guard had over-extended himself, but it still drove nearly all of the sensation—save for overwhelming pain—from Humph's arm. *Hope it was worth it, bought Fred some time, maybe.* For now, he had to focus on his own attacker; the guard was pressing his advantage, trying to catch Humph on his arm again, soften him up for the finish. Humph ducked under one swing that the guard misjudged, going wide; the Boggart used his good arm to shove the guard in the back, sending him face first into a wall. He tried to unholster the revolver, but the guard had recovered enough to kick him squarely in the side, causing him to fumble and send the gun clattering to the floor

"I'm getting sick of this shit!" These guys definitely had been trained against Paras. They weren't making most of the usual Norm mistakes. Humph threw himself at the guard just as the guard was springing off of the wall; they met in the middle of the hallway, colliding hard enough to almost drive the wind out of Humph's lungs. He tried to claw the bastard's kidneys out, but the uniform the man was wearing wasn't giving; some sort of tear-resistant armor, at the very least. Whoever the bastards were behind all of this, they trained *and* equipped their goons to deal with Para powers. Humph didn't have time to process the new information; the guard was at his throat again. The fight went to the floor, both of them trying to get a few good hits on the other. Humph heard more than he saw Fred wolf out; he didn't know how much good that was going to do. The hallway was too cramped with all four of them wrestling around; Humph reared a fist back to punch his guard, only to accidentally smash his fist into Fred's nose. The blow elicited an angry snarl from the Were, but he kept fighting.

The guard was good, too damned good; he flipped his legs around, changing the center of gravity for the both of them. From there, he was able to slip under and around Humph, flipping him over. At that point, the guard was on top of Humph; the Boggart barely had time to catch the guard's wrists as a knife came down toward his throat. *Where the hell did he get that from?* The guard was putting his full weight down, trying to drive the knife through the Boggart's voicebox and into the vicinity of his spine. Humph noticed, in one of those surreal moments of clarity that happen when adrenaline starts flowing, that the guard's ID badge was hanging from his lapel. Taking a chance, Humph used one hand to rip the badge off, while working one of his legs between them until he had a foot braced against the man's belly. The knife was moving down, centimeter by centimeter.

"Fred! Throw your guy, now!" With a final burst of effort, Humph kicked the guard off of him; a testament to the man's reflexes, he landed on his feet, already in a fighting stance. He didn't have tunnel-vision, either; the guard was able to catch his colleague as Fred, reluctant to miss an opportunity to savage a deserving opponent but still cognizant enough to follow his partner's instructions, threw the other guard. Somehow, as he passed, the Boggart snagged his ID off his shirt too. Both guards retrieved their firearms, aiming at Fred and Humph as they got to their feet.

"Hands in the air, now!" Both guards had self-satisfied smirks on their faces; even consummate professionals can get full of themselves after getting the drop on an opponent.

"Whatever you say, pal." Humph complied, looking over to Fred; the Were's features were returning to normal.

"I hope you know what the hell you're doing, dumbass," Fred sneered. His expression immediately changed when they heard the ultrasonic whine of an energy weapon powering up behind them. The smirks the guards had disappeared.

"I do; now duck!"

They both threw themselves to the floor; Humph shut his eyes and covered his head, and Fred followed suit. No sooner had they hit the floor than both of them felt intense heat on their backs, and smelled the unmistakable acrid tang of ozonating air, accompanied by what sounded like a very sharp and electrical *zat!* When they looked up, where the two guards used to be there were two vaguely humanoid shapes burnt black, along with a very dark smear against the floor and wall. Upon closer inspection, the bodies looked more like piles of heavily burnt wood, although they stank of burned meat.

Humph stood up, nursing his injured forearm. Over his shoulder, the security bots were settling back down into inactivity. Fred looked at him, uncomprehending.

"Never leave home without your plastic," Humph said, holding up the ID badges of the guards. "Let's get out of here. Now."

Understanding dawned on Fred's face. "You've got it, boss. My fire should start in earnest any—"

There was a muffled *whumph* in the distance. Alarms were going off, but...it seemed haphazard, as if they were only local. Then there was a bigger *whumph*, and the two of them felt a pressure-wave pass through the corridor. The security bots came to life again, and headed in the direction of Maintenance.

And all down the corridor, doors began springing open on their own, and people began pouring into the corridor. Fred found a knot of people in lab coats and joined them; Humph did the same, but not before scooping up his revolver and surreptitiously reholstering it.

There was a kind of stuttering *blat* from whatever they were using for a speaker system, and finally the real alarms kicked on. Humph guessed that someone had triggered it from the security desk manually. More security bots were pressed against the wall, edging their way back toward the direction of the fire, contrary to the streams of increasingly panicking workers. When they reached the entrance, Humph noticed the elderly security guard standing next to his desk, looking bewildered. On an impulse he couldn't have explained, Humph grabbed him by the collar and dragged him out the exit with everyone else. The smoke was really starting to pour out of the doors in huge billowing, acrid clouds; some of the windows further back in the facility had flames visible through them.

The crowd of lab technicians and office workers had gathered out in front of the building, and were milling around. "What happened?" The security guard was shaking his head slowly, looking back at the inferno that was his job just minutes ago.

"Sorry, old timer. Time to look for a new gig." Humph looked for Fred in the crowd; the Were was already by a aircar that had stopped, the owner having exited his vehicle to gaze at the fire. One thing that never went to waste in a neighborhood like this was the opportunity to enjoy a good building fire, especially if it wasn't your building. Humph wove his way through the crowd, sparing a final glance over his shoulder as he reached the aircar and Fred. The old timer was pointing at him insistently. *Uh oh.*

"Those two! Somebody stop them!" The old security guard was shouting loud enough for the on-site security to hear over the noise of the crowd. Humph noticed with dismay that they all turned to focus their collective attention on him and Fred; they all started to move toward the pair, with one talking urgently into a comm device.

"Like you said, boss, it's time to go!" Fred hopped into the passenger side of the aircar, slamming the door behind him. Humph followed suit on the opposite side; the original owner finally noticed what was happening, but only had time to futilely pound on the driver-side window before the vehicle lurched into the sky. "Think we got away clean?"

"Not a chance. Our luck has been shit lately."

"Well...there's this much. No way they can cover up all those bodies in the back room once the Fire Service gets there." Fred's face was fixed in a snarl.

"You're an optimist, Fred. I'm not putting anything past the bunch of bastards that want us dead. You saw that shit in there; they're doing something to kill Weres. Chemical? Biological?" Humph shook his head. "That's beyond serious; that sort of research carries the death penalty, never mind using test subjects like that."

The rattle of bullets pinging off the roof of the aircar interrupted any further speculation. One of the rounds that penetrated passed close enough to whisper past Humph's cheek; Fred wasn't as lucky, with a round hitting him in the shoulder.

"Fuck!" He frantically started digging at the wound, using two claws to pull the slug out; it was sizzling with his blood on it. "Silver! They aren't playing around, boss." With the silver removed, his wound started to close up, the process sped up by his supernatural healing. "What's the plan now?"

Humph took out his revolver and tossed it into Fred's lap. "Shoot back, damnit! I'll try to lose them. Don't lean out too far, though; it's a long way to the ground."

Humph wondered if their pursuers might be more careful about their shots if there were more civilians around. That was an evil thought, yes. But he was no angel, and after seeing those piled up bodies back at the lab, he knew for a fact that it was back to the bad old days, of Para versus Norm, at least in *someone's* eyes, and that same someone was behind whoever was pulling the trigger now. Time to play dirty. *Just the way I like it.*

He arced the car around, heading away from the industrial area and straight into residential. *Ideally* it would have been expensive, exclusive residential, but there wasn't much of that around on Mildred. Common-block high-rises, whose grimy exterior reminded him of long-ago days in Chicago, would have to do. The nice thing was that a lot of those high-rises were parked really close together. There was room for an aircar, but not much more.

Oh, what I wouldn't give for a dragon wingman about now. Fred punched out the glass of the window behind him, then leaned out of the door with one arm wrapped around the post, firing carefully. "I hope you got more ammo for this thing, boss," he snarled into the wind. His face was half feral now; probably adrenaline.

"Cantrip," Humph shouted back. "Self-replacing slug in the last chamber. Just a plain-Jane lead slug, though."

"They're fracking Norms. Lead'll frack 'em up just fine." Fred really was in a rage. "*Die*, you murderous bastards!" Fred plugged away with the revolver, emptying it at the pursuing aircar as it swooped down behind them. When he finally reached the last chamber, he held out his hand for reloads; Humph quickly handed him three speedloaders, dividing his attention between that and driving. Even with the cantrip, it was more convenient and faster to use reloads instead of having to manually rotate the cylinder to reach the last chamber every time. At the rate that Fred was burning through the ammunition, it wouldn't be long before he had to resort to the cantrip to keep shooting.

Humph spotted just what he was looking for; two high-rises with a narrow passage between them. Someone was about to get a show. The passage was big enough for the air-car—barely. He had no idea about the size of what was behind him.

More bullets pinged off the vehicle, as their pursuers realized where he was heading. "Pull your head in!" he yelled at Fred, who did a quick look-ahead and pulled in faster than a turtle taking shelter. Then they were in the slot.

To Humph's acute disappointment, there was no *boom* behind them of the pursuit vehicle hitting one or both walls. Instead he caught a glimpse of them pulling straight up just short of the slot.

Well, that would gain them a little time and distance....

To cement that, he dove as he exited, doing a dance around shorter buildings at about the three-story-height level. The more he could confuse their pursuers when they came back down and around the high-rise, the better.

"Where'd you learn to fly like this?" Fred shouted over the wind rushing through the broken-out windows. He leaned out slightly to look behind them, watching for pursuit.

"World War Two. Long story."

"You'll have to tell it to me some—look out!" Fred barely had time to duck fully back into the car before the pursuit vehicle slammed into them from above, partially crumpling the roof.

So, they were swapping out bullets for ramming. In theory that was less hazardous for the innocent bystanders. In practice though, an aircar on fire hitting an apartment block would not be good for anyone. *Maybe they're as fed up with this chase business as I am; if they get a good hit on us in the works of this jalopy, we're landing—hard.* The thought was punctuated with another jarring crash as the security car rammed them again, trying to force them to the ground; with the buildings on either side, there wasn't very much room to maneuver.

It seemed that the same potential disaster had finally occurred to the other pilots—or maybe whoever was controlling them had figured out that a fiery crash into the side of a heavily occupied building was going to become a nightmare *nothing* could cover up. The two security cars were maneuvering to force Humph and Fred to the ground. Presumably it wouldn't matter if they crashed, as long as they didn't take anyone with them.

Now what Humph had to do instead of dodging bullets was to dodge in and out of the spaces between the apartment buildings so that only one of the aircars could get on top of him at any one time. *His* goal was to get above them; two could play their game, and if he could force one of *them* into the ground, the odds would even up.

Their handicap was that this was a civilian car. Their pursuers'…wasn't. Armoring, heavier and with no speed limiters. He had to do a lot with braking. Fortunately, he'd learned his craft on prop-planes, which were a lot less forgiving than these glorified shuttles. He'd done dogfighting, for real, with machine-guns stitching their way across his wings. They'd likely only trained on simulators.

He got his chance when he managed to brake unexpectedly and dart upwards while he and one of the two security cars were in another slot between two buildings. There was no place for the security car to go. He dropped down on the top of it like a rock, and accelerated, forcing it down before the pilot had time to react. *This* wasn't the sort of thing you got with simulator training. The two of them powered toward a parking lot, and the heavier engine on the security car was not able to prevail against the weight of two cars, the force Humph was applying and pitiless gravity. At the last possible second, Humph pulled their car up. The engine screamed for mercy but obeyed. It was too late for the security car; all that armor told against it. The security car made a barely-controlled crash, skidding across the paved area rather than slamming into it. But it couldn't avoid the knot of parked cars ahead of it, and it did slam into them in a shower of glass and metal fragments.

One down. One to go. "Fred, is there any way for you to get the civilian limiters off this thing?" he shouted over the wind roaring in through the broken windows. If they could disable the limiters, it would open up Humph's options for speed and maneuverability; by law, all civilian and commercial aircars were made virtually idiot-proof to keep the airways from becoming free-for-all destruction derbies.

"Not unless you want to die in a horrible crash," Fred replied, snarling at the mess of crashed cars and the wobbly figures pulling themselves out of the security car. "It requires being on the ground and powered down, you big dope. And even if it didn't, I'm not climbing out on the hood right now, thanks."

Well so much for that idea. This last security car wasn't taking any chances with Humph, and this chase couldn't go on forever. Sooner or later—probably sooner—they'd get backup or be able to ground the aircar, and that would be all she wrote. He couldn't high-tail back to the others; leading whoever was pulling the strings on this game back to Harry would get all of them killed, and not all that pleasantly or quickly. Humph made a snap decision, then started peeling his jacket off.

"I'm going to try something. It probably won't work, but it's our only shot." He handed the jacket to Fred, focusing on driving while he talked. "Once I get low, you've gotta bail; find cover. My jacket has the last of the reloads for the pistol. No matter what happens, get back to the others. They've gotta know about what we found in that lab. I'm betting you and Jim can figure out ways to get it out to the Furs at least, if not the rest of the semi-civilized universe. Got that?"

"Yeah, boss, but...what the hell are you going to try?"

"Something incredibly stupid. Par for the course, right?"

"At least you're consistent, boss." Fred bundled the jacket up, tucking it under his arm. Checking the revolver a final time to make sure it was ready, he nodded to Humph. "I'm set, boss."

Fred was, at heart, an engineer, not an action hero. Humph was going to have to give him instructions for this. "When I'm close enough to the ground and going slow enough that you think you can survive it, I want you to jump out, roll and get under cover." He glanced over at Fred. "You might want to wolf-out for that."

"But—"

"Don't argue, just do it." With one eye on the sky, Humph dove for the deck and began maneuvering around obstacles among the buildings. Fred went half-wolf rather than full wolf, but everything Humph knew about Furs told him that would give him just about all of the healing ability of the fully lupine form and none of the disadvantages. Fred didn't bother opening what was left of the door; he just kicked it off its hinges, grabbed the A and B pillars, and poised on the edge. He must have spotted a good opening as Humph streaked down an alley, just above a lot of dumpsters laden with what looked like industrial stuff. One second he was there in the doorframe; the next, he was gone.

"Here goes nothing," Humph muttered, gunning the throttle.

Fred landed hard, trying to roll with the impact and failing. The result was that after tumbling over trash and broken crap he ground to a halt, the last foot of it on his face. He hardly felt the road rash, though; with the adrenaline and being partially wolfed out, he was back up on his feet and dashing for cover immediately. A dumpster that was still smoldering from being used as an impromptu burn-pit was the first thing that he found; he thudded his back against the side of it, crouching down.

Humph had laid on some extra speed after swooping back into the air, but he was coming to the end of the alley. There wasn't going to be any room left to run, soon. Fred first heard, then saw the pursuing aircar as it zoomed overhead. He did his best to work his way into a corner between the dumpster and the wall it was nestled against; the last thing he needed was for one of the security goons in that car to fill him with more precious metal. *C'mon, boss, whatever you're going to pull out of your sleeve, now's the time.*

As if answering Fred's call, Humph fishtailed the aircar at the very end of the alley; it was close enough that he could clearly see sparks lighting off of the rear of the vehicle as it scraped against concrete. As soon as he was righted, Humph floored the aircar; the engine whined in protest, but obediently responded and was going its maximum speed within seconds. The security aircar matched speed, facing the hopeless charge. Fred cried out wordlessly, jumping up and lining up Humph's Webley-Fosbery with the aircar; it felt as if it weighed a ton, and that he was moving in slow motion. He knew what was going to happen, and had to do something, anything, to stop it. It was already too late, however; both cars were well out of range of the revolver, at least with how bad Fred's aim was. All Fred could do was watch as the two vehicles hurtled toward each other. At the last second, the security car tried to swerve out of the way, but there was nowhere to go in the alley. The aircars impacted with a sickening and too-loud crunch, immediately followed by the percussive beat and pressure wave from an explosion as their engines and fuel tanks detonated.

Harry paced around the bunker restlessly. He had been ignoring Lori almost completely since Humph and Fred had left. She had stayed in the main compartment, watching the entrance and waiting. Jim was still busy, working on something at his computer terminal. Whenever Harry tried to ask him a question, the Zombie simply replied with a grunt or a single word. They were all nervous, and were doing their best to hide it with varying levels of success. He desperately wanted to be doing something other than sitting around in this warren. He couldn't even seem to think in this hole; the lighting or just the tight spaces or Lori sitting there sort of distracting him, something was sapping his ability to concentrate, to make himself useful. *If only I could get a latte, or some room service. Maybe one of my suits. That'd clear my head.*

This entire episode had almost driven him to his wits' end; if he wasn't being dragged somewhere, he was being shot at. If he wasn't being shot at, he was running. If he wasn't running, he was hiding, and so on. It was enough to cause any sensible and sophisticated person to go insane. Despite all of that, he was starting to get into what he saw as the spirit of things. This was an *adventure*; not one of the lame, bought-and-paid-for trips that some of the more eccentric guests at the parties he attended would brag about. Holidays where they shot renowned and dangerous game on very carefully cultivated and sanitized hunting preserves, or "adventure cruises," sailing or flying into situations like planetary storms or massive volcanic eruptions that gave the illusion of peril but where no one was in danger of so much as a hangnail. This was *real*. They could all be caught and killed at any moment, and he was at the center of it. In one of his rare moments of clarity, Harry realized that he was probably the happiest he had been in a long time, never mind the fact that a well-equipped and well-funded group of merciless killers wanted to turn him to dust.

*When this is over….*Well that was the question, wasn't it? It might be over with him dead, but if it wasn't, what was he going to do with the rest of his life? This was the first time he'd ever been this close to Paras for this long, and he kind of liked it. *They* were more real than any of his so-called friends. If he went back to his old sort of life…*I'll be bored out of my skull.*

Before Harry could ponder that line of thought any further, he heard the tell-tale screech of the exterior hatch opening. Harry and Lori looked at each other, then at Jim. None of them had heard the passcode they had all agreed on for anyone re-entering the bunker. There was a quick scramble for weapons, everyone trying to be as quiet as possible; Jim had thrown his helmet on and picked up a pipe, while Lori had produced a long knife seemingly from thin air. Harry twisted around, unable to find anything, and then stood in the center of the room, with a deer-in-the-headlights look plastered on his face.

Jim took pity on him and threw a broom at him just as the footfalls reached the inner door. Harry fumbled with the broom, sending it twirling in the air as he tried to get a grip on it. The final hatch swung open. It wasn't a squad of mercenaries with guns at the ready. Just Fred, looking a little worse for the wear but otherwise fine.

The tension in the room broke, with Harry the first one to speak.

"Holy crap, Fred. Way to give a body a scare, huh?" He bent down to pick up the broom, leaning on it and doing his best to strike a manly pose. "I mean, we were prepared for any sort of violent encounter, but still, you mustn't enter so abruptly and without announcing yourself; wouldn't want the women to faint, right?" He grinned, looking back at Jim. The Zombie had removed his helmet, setting it down on the desk in front of him. Once Harry saw the stricken gaze on Jim's emaciated face, his own expression soon fell.

"Fred," Jim said slowly, something strange in his voice. "Where's Humph?"

"Gone," was the only thing that Fred could manage to say. He was holding what looked like Humph's jacket; Harry's gaze drifted down to the revolver stuck into Fred's waistband. He heard a slight rustling of fabric on fabric behind him. When he turned around, Lori was already walking toward the door, the few things she owned in her bag. Her face was a mask of tears, but she was walking determinedly.

"Lori, please, just wait—" She silently pushed past Harry, then Fred, and then she was gone out the door without a single word. Just like that, just as suddenly and irrevocably as

Humph, Lori was now gone. Harry knew that she wouldn't be back, no matter how much he wished for it. He decided that maybe he didn't like this adventure business all that much after all.

The three of them were silent for a long time, as if they were frozen in place where they each stood in the bunker. The thought floated through Harry's mind that maybe if they were still enough, time would freeze too, maybe turn back and then Humph would still be alive.

"…the main thing is to get it all out to the Fur Dens," Fred said, for about the fifth time. "After that, we try and get it to the Fang Hives. We let *them* work the media; there are enough of them that whoever this is won't be able to stop them all."

Inside information? Wishful thinking? Skinny Jim wasn't sure which…but he did figure this much: "Whoever" was behind all of this, their adversaries were probably betting that now that their ragtag band of brothers had discovered just what was being covered up, and had gotten footage of it (which he had, via the spy-cam he'd glued into Fred's hair right at the hairline), they'd go straight to the media themselves. So Fred's plan made perfect sense.

Harry wasn't buying it, though. It was too easy, too perfect. Something they could have conceivably done a while ago. Before Humph had…gone. Fred was repeating himself too much, as if he was trying to convince himself a little too hard as much as the rest of them. They were silent in the aircar for some time, all of them uncomfortable and distinctly aware of it. Harry cleared his throat twice before speaking. "I know that we're not going to spill the story, not the way you two are talking about." The long pause when neither Fred nor Jim denied the statement seemed to bolster Harry, shore up his courage. "You're going to trade me in to save yourselves, aren't you?"

The Adjudicator was satisfied with himself. He had a real name, of course, but his own ego-mania sometimes overflowed into reality; most of his underlings were just as ruthless as he was, but few of them dared to call him anything other than by his self-styled title for fear of what he would do to them. He was a cruel man, a sadist, and only took joy when someone else was submitting to his will. Pain, terror, and violence were his favorite and most-used tools. Paired with that willingness to inflict hurt into the world was a cunning intelligence, cold and sharp. Without his mind he would have been just an average bully; someone to watch out for, but easily lost in multitudes. But he wasn't the average bully; he was able to hide his cruelties, his excesses. His career afforded him all the opportunities he could ever want to kill and maim, all of it sanctioned and generously funded. It was good to be a government man.

This job was no different, really, than the dozens he'd had before it. Someone had done something or found something that they shouldn't have; they had become an impediment to the smooth workings of the machine, and thus had to be removed. That's where the Adjudicator came in; to turn the handle and grind whoever was between the gears. This time, it was a minor socialite; one Harry Somerfield. He was connected, but no one was above being dealt with when it came to the Adjudicator and those whose interests he protected. Mr. Somerfield had enlisted some help along the way; minor annoyances like that sometimes happened with a job, but that was part of the fun. The chase was part of what kept the Adjudicator hungry and interested; flushing his quarry out, and the attendant violence, all sated his bloodlust little by little until the very end.

It seemed that the end was fast approaching for Mr. Somerfield. Two of his compatriots had sold him out, and were now on their way to deliver the playboy in exchange for their lives. It always came down to something like this, with this sort of scum; begging and pleading, giving each other up for even a few more minutes of their pathetic lives. He had been hoping that he would be able to run down the entire mangy lot; seeing the realization on their faces when their little "deal" would prove futile would be almost as satisfying. Their naiveté was almost funny; after the little stunt they had pulled at the production lab, and then, the number of his underlings they'd taken out in that chase, how could they think that they'd ever be allowed to live? *You don't fuck with the government; we're here to fuck with you.*

The Adjudicator didn't waste much time pondering the concerns of soon-to-be-dead freaks; they would arrive soon enough, and then the real fun could begin. The only question that remained was how long he would take to kill them; such things had to be done with a measure of artistry to really be enjoyed.

This was not Fred's favorite part of Mildred. Even fully wolfed-out, he never came here unless he was forced to.

Sunset City Recreational Park; well, the name was apt if you considered that the place had been "sunsetted" years ago. Another victim of in a long line of budget cuts, it was not situated in a commercially advantageous spot, so Sunset City—a subdivision comprised of mostly low-income highrises inhabited by low-income renters—had neither sold the land nor bothered to maintain it. The original plan had probably been for a "wilderness-style" park combined with a big, grassy commons and other amenities, along the lines of Central Park in New York City on Old Earth. Now the grassy commons was waist-high in weeds, the trails among the dense trees were the hunting grounds of predators with two, four, and six legs, the ball parks could only be discerned by the remains of chain-link fences full of blown trash, and the entire 80-acre site gave off the aura of something just after an apocalypse, poisoned and abused nature struggling to reclaim the landscape. Fred knew of some packs who hunted here recreationally...they would never say *what* it was that they hunted, and he never asked. Suffice it to say that anyone here after dark was probably someone who would not be missed.

Jim and Fred had Harry sandwiched in between them as they waded through weeds and garbage to what had been a band shell. Well, it was still a band shell; plascreet was hard to destroy with anything less than a pocket nuke or specialized construction equipment. But it had been stripped of anything that could be sold or just pried off, so the doors on either side where musicians would have entered and exited were open holes like a pair of gouged-out eyes. And it had been graffitied up as far as anyone could reach, and then a little higher. Someone had been ambitious and brought a rope or a ladder…or else the rumors of Were-apes were real, and they liked to tag buildings.

In the half-light of near dusk, the selection of dark-suited men waiting on the plascreet stage looked even more out of place than they might have in full light. In daylight, they could have been mistaken for a group of entrepreneurs examining the area for potential, or even city officials surveying the damage. But now, so close to dark, there was no reason for anyone dressed as they were to be in a place this dangerous.

Unless these wolves-in-sheep's-clothing happened to be even more dangerous than the killers that called this place their territory.

Dead center in front of the congregation was the apparent leader; he was in a suit just like the rest, though his was plainly more expensive and actually tailored. He could have been anywhere between his late twenties and early fifties; he had a timeless look to him, and by all common aesthetic standards should have been attractive, or at the very least, ordinary. There was something…off about him, however. Maybe it was something about the eyes, or the constant half-smile he always had on his face. It was a strange sort of vibe, unwholesome, like the feeling one would get from being around a convicted but unrepentant child molester.

Harry hung his head, listlessly being led on. Jim and Fred exchanged a look with each other before they continued toward the waiting team, coming up around fifty paces short of the stage before the leader spoke.

"That'll be far enough, gentlemen." The sound was carried easily by the acoustics of the stage, and none of them were forced to shout as they talked. The leader kept his hands behind his back as he talked, looking down on the trio, still smirking. "You," he nodded to Jim, "can remove that helmet, if you like. I don't believe that there'll be any need to keep up appearances here."

Jim let go of Harry's arm to use both hands, removing his helmet. None of the suited goons on the stage seemed to be surprised to see that he was a Reboot. "You sure seem to know a lot about us."

"It's my job to find out such things. And to find people once they've been…misplaced."

Fred took a step forward. "We've fulfilled our end of the bargain. We've brought Harry to you. In exchange, we get to walk away from this. That's our deal."

"That is what was discussed." The leader raised a hand; the men behind him all produced compact and rather dangerous-looking weapons on command, aiming them directly at the trio.

Fred's hackles raised, and he started to slowly unsheathe his claws, the beginning stage of him wolfing-out. "What the hell is this?"

"The arrangement that we discussed, whereby you go free in exchange for turning over Harry Somerfield to us, is predicated upon, first, us actually needing to let you go. Most importantly, however, it assumes you actually have Harry Somerfield. Which you clearly do not."

Fred literally jumped, he was so startled. "What in hell are you talking about?" he demanded. "He's right here!" And with that, he shoved Harry forward, making him stumble a little.

"Drop the act, please. It's starting to get pathetic." The Chief Goon—Fred could only think of him as that—lifted his lip in a sneer. Fred looked back at Harry, distraught. This was all falling apart! This wasn't in the plan! Now what was he going to do?

"It's okay, Fred." Harry stood up straighter, looking into the leader's eyes. "There's more to this guy than meets the eye." As he spoke, he walked forward a few paces. His features started to change; his face darkened, he shrank and became more compact and wiry, and short, bristly black hair sprouted on the exposed parts of his body. Once he was done, he was Harry no more. Humph planted his fists on his hips, sizing up the goons. "How'd you know, if I may ask?"

The leader tapped the side of his head with a finger. "Having money affords one all the best toys; even ones that can pierce your glamour." He started forward a few steps, still smiling. "To be honest, we thought you were dead in the collision. I didn't know that you were alive until your friends came strolling along with you in tow, instead of Mr. Somerfield." The leader sounded mildly impressed. "My turn to ask how you managed that. If I may?"

Humph held up his pocket watch. "You have your tricks, I have mine. Slipped this into a jacket that I gave Fred right before he bailed out. Effectively teleported to it right before the collision; that way it looks like I got crushed on all the cameras. Figured it'd give us an edge, you thinking I was dead." The leader watched Humph replace the pocket watch, still smirking.

"It would have been a good deception, had it worked. But to what end?"

Humph shrugged. "Couldn't let you have the kid. He's dumb, and out of his league, but he doesn't deserve what you bastards were going to do to him. Plus," Humph leaned forward slightly, "I figured I could twist your head off and shove it up your ass, if I could just get close enough."

"Very cute, Mr. Boggart." The leader was allowing a tinge of annoyance to creep into his voice. "None of you are going to leave here alive, you know. If you'd like the small mercy of dying quicker than the others, I do suggest you tell me where Mr. Somerfield is."

Humph thought for a moment. "First, I've got to know something." The leader waved his hand for Humph to continue. "Why Weres? Why go after them? What the hell did the Fur set ever do to you? Piss on your shrubs?" *Keep monologuing, you rat fuck, and I'll waltz right up and gut you where you stand.* Humph continued to slowly walk forward, keeping his hands at his sides and his posture non-threatening.

The leader laughed; it was a sharp, mean sound without any real mirth in it. "You really have no clue how far off the beaten path you've stumbled, Mr. Boggart. The Weres are just a small part of things. A side show for the main attraction, the big event. In time—" Floodlights suddenly hit the leader, his men on the stage, and Humph. Everyone looked around, shielding their eyes. Humph saw a flash of panic cross the leader's face; things were finally not going according to plan for *him*, instead of not for everyone else.

About damn time.

"*This is the MPPF. Throw down your weapons and remain where you are. Anyone that attempts to flee or resist will be engaged immediately with lethal force. This is your only warning.*" Then Humph saw them: at least four specialized aircars, huge ones, painted solid black. Ah, the glory of fully stealthed aircars. Nothing to give them away until they were all in place and there was nowhere to run to and nowhere to hide. They didn't have any markings, and dozens of troops in tactical gear were rappelling out of the open doors. Good move, that; kept the aircars as overhead support while the troops piled onto the ground. Humph approved; this was the first time he was actually happy to see the cops.

"Kill them, kill them all!" The leader of the goons shouted furiously at his men, pulling out his own sidearm. Then the shooting began; the goons, the leader, and the newly arrived troops.

Skinny Jim jammed his helmet back on; at that point, Humph knew, he was the next thing to invulnerable in his robot shell. He might *look* like a battered old bot, but that chassis was from an industrial model and was hardened against damn near anything. Fred wasted no time, and wolfed out partly; that would take care of ordinary projectiles and even direct energy weapons up to a point, but not silver. Humph was the one who was the most vulnerable.

But he was also the one who was the most angry.

Both of his partners charged forward toward the goons; it was time for payback, time for blood on the ground. Humph looked for the leader; he was still standing out in the open, firing at the aircars. When he stopped to reload, both of them locked eyes. Humph unholstered the old Webley-Fosbery from under Harry's rumpled suit jacket, and ran toward the leader. The bastard wasn't smiling anymore. Just as Humph raised his revolver, the leader turned to run, darting between his men with bullets and energy blasts hitting the ground around him.

I am not letting this son of a bitch get away!

The Boggart ran after the leader, his legs pumping hard and driving him forward as fast as they could carry him.

Some of the goons tried to stop him, tried to run interference for their boss. He shot the first one squarely in the face, not even breaking stride. The second one stepped in front of his path; a backhanded pistol strike to his orbital socket sent the man down the ground, maybe dead. Humph vaulted over the body, still following the leader. Off to the side of the fighting, he saw Jim knock down two goons, messily kicking in their heads after they were sent sprawling to the ground. Energy blasts and bullets ricocheted off of his robot shell, with some of the shots getting sent off wildly, one of them striking a goon square in the back. In the back of his mind, he found himself marveling; when he'd first hooked up with these two, he would never have dreamed of seeing the Reboot wade into a fight like this. Fred—well, the guy might be an engineer, but he was also a Fur—a tough Loner at that—and Furs, no matter what they had been before they were Turned, were scrappers. But a Reboot? Normally they won—back when they were still hostile—by sheer overwhelming numbers. And that had been back when they weren't manual labor, and had to kill for their food. You just didn't picture them duking it out, Boggart-style.

He emptied the rest of his revolver's cylinder into the gut of a suited goon who had grabbed hold of his shoulder, costing him precious steps and time. He turned, trying to catch up with the leader; he had to get him. If that bastard got away, this would never be over. He got a glimpse of the leader sprinting down a side path, and took off after him. Just as he was about to reach the beginning of the path, four goons, all with their guns trained on him, closed ranks, blocking him off from his quarry.

Humph raised his revolver, pulling the trigger—*click*. He hadn't had time to reload, and he couldn't cock the mechanism and pull the trigger fast enough to get to the last cylinder again for the cantrip to kick in; at least not enough times to take out all four of the goons. They were about to cut him down when an inhuman howl split the sky, cutting through the noise of the melee. A large auburn blur bathed in silver light slammed into all four of the goons, dragging them screaming to the ground. Fred—he was in full form, centered in the middle of a moonglow-spot trained on him from one of the aircars—had the men pinned down, and was literally tearing them apart before Humph's eyes. This wasn't the half-form he could take at will. This was the Monster In The Dark, the fully feral Beast for whom killing was as easy as breathing. Easier. His victims really never had a chance.

They weren't dying quietly. The werewolf's head came up, gore dripping from his muzzle. Humph saw a glimmer of intelligence behind those canine eyes, and what he would have sworn was a wink; with that, the Were was back up and looking for more victims. Humph had heard of the spotlights, restricted to law enforcement, but he'd never seen what happened when one hit a Fur until now. The difference between a moonspot and a real full moon was that the Fur in question would keep his human brain rather than going completely mindless and bestial. How they managed *that*, Humph had no idea. *I'm going to owe Fred a case of scotch for that save. Business first, though.* Humph ran down the path, doggedly following the leader.

The path was overgrown, with branches hanging down from trees and bushes growing out into the middle from the edges. The leader of the goons would wait at some of the twists and turns, shooting at Humph when he came into view; Humph had had time to reload at this point, and shot back. He took his time, lining up his sights and squeezing the trigger. During the last exchange, he saw his round take the leader in the knee; a spurt of blood and the man's cry of pain confirmed the wound. The leader kept stumbling down the path, fumbling with his pistol and cursing. Humph slowed down, from a trot to finally walking, as he followed the blood on the ground. The path terminated at a stone arch bridge; it must have been part of a scenic overlook for the river it crossed over, which ended with a gentle waterfall to the left. The leader paused on the bridge, still trying to reload his sidearm. Finally he jammed the magazine home, raising the pistol; Humph did the same, firing once. The bullet caught the leader in his shoulder, causing him to drop his pistol and fall back over the edge of the bridge. He landed with a small splash in the river which wasn't anything more than ornamental. He came out of the water gasping and floundering toward the waterfall; not dead yet, evidently. Humph followed him, still unhurried; when he reached the bridge, he walked around it and into the river. The water wasn't very deep even at the center, maybe a foot at most.

The leader reached the waterfall, then struggled to stand up; there wasn't anywhere else for him to go. The waterfall fell onto a shallow artificial lake, which was thickly overgrown and green with algae from lack of care. There were jagged rocks at the bottom of the waterfall, nearly forty feet down. He turned to face Humph, clutching his shoulder. "You goddamned mongrel!" Spittle leaked down his chin as he shouted. "You think this is the end? You think that killing me is going to change anything, anything at all?" Humph holstered his pistol as he trudged through the water. He walked right up to the leader, staring him in the eyes right up until he plunged his claws into the man's belly.

"No, I don't think it'll bring back all of my friends that you've murdered, or change anything else that has happened. But killing you is too damned satisfying to pass up." He dug the claws in further, twisting to the side and upward, the fabric of the man's shirt and suit bunching up in between Humph's knuckles. The leader's eyes bulged out of his skull, his mouth ringed in a silent "oh" of agony. Humph used his free hand to shove the leader, hard, pulling him off of Humph's claws and sending him over the edge of the waterfall. There was a loud clap as he impacted with the rocks below.

Humph looked over the edge. The man wasn't moving, wasn't breathing. Still.

The Boggart selected a good-sized rock from the ornamental boulders in the stream. Fortunately, they hadn't been cemented into place. He picked it up with a grunt, walked carefully to the edge of the waterfall, aimed, and threw.

It landed with a wet *smack* on the human's head.

No sooner had it done so, than there was movement in the underbrush. First one, then a second, then a third and a fourth ghoul crept out from cover on all fours. In a moment there was nothing of the body to be seen beneath the feeding ghouls. Humph didn't bother to watch any further, opting to wash the blood off of his hands in the river before walking back to the path. "*Now* there's no chance of seeing that prick again. Rot in hell, asshole."

"I don't get it," said Harry, as he handed Humph a double scotch. "What the *hell* were they after?"

"Captain Monologue didn't get to finish," Humph replied, taking his first sip and savoring it. "And once the fighting started, and he knew the jig was up, well, you wouldn't have gotten anything out of him with pliers and razor blades. At least, nothing useful."

He'd seen the type before, and although he wasn't going to let Harry in on the full deal, he recognized a government goon when he saw one. Even if the Chief Suit *hadn't* been conditioned to a fare-thee-well to resist torture and other interrogation techniques—and Humph strongly doubted that he hadn't been—he'd probably been implanted with a remote device to eliminate him if he was "compromised." Probably without his knowledge, during something like minor surgery or dental work, long long before he ever reached the position he'd held. The man himself had said it: Someone was playing a long game.

The less Harry knew about this, the better off Harry was. He'd done all right for a green kid, but they'd had craptons of luck on their side. The playboy would be no match even for one of The Suit's underlings, much less whoever had been pulling The Suit's strings. All the same, he'd come through for them. When Harry thought he was being sold out so that Jim and Fred could save their own hides, he was actually being taken to meet the still-alive-and-pissed-off Humph so that they could make a switch. Humph impersonating Harry would give him enough time to get back to his mother; with her seeing him alive and hearing the story straight from him, they figured that she could pull some strings and maybe get them out of the jam. Mrs. Somerfield had, and then some. Humph could only guess how. It could be that renegade lab massacring Furs wasn't the only time the firm had done business with the government. Or it could be Mrs. Somerfield just happened to have some powerful pals. You never know when an old college friend is going to come in handy.

After Humph had given the hard goodbye to the lead goon, he had made his way back to the stage where the bulk of the fighting had taken place. By the time he got back, everything was just about said and done; Fred was back to Norm and wrapped in a blanket due to his clothes being shredded. Jim was doing his best deaf-mute impression next to Fred, pretending to only respond to Fred's voice like a real bot would. None of the goons were alive; between Fred, Jim, and the late arrivals, not a single one of them had made it. Humph suspected that the "cops" had performed a few executions when no one was looking. He had taken a chance and talked to the one who seemed to be in charge. The Boggart had dealt with all sorts of law enforcement over the years, for various reasons. One thing he was sure of was that that guy was *not* a cop. On the other hand, Fred hadn't been the only Fur on the ground in that crew, every one of those aircars had a moonspot and there had been at least four others in the wrecking crew besides Fred. So at least they were Para-friendly. When he hazarded asking the Norm who he worked for, the man only smiled sadly and said, "You wouldn't have heard of us."

After that, everything went as Humph had expected. Everyone was told to shut up, and forget ever being there. The warrant for Humph's arrest was dropped, and everything was swept under the rug. Fred was not happy about it at all, and understandably so. Humph had been able to talk him out of going public with info of what went down. From what Jim had been able to piece together after the fact, once the office was back in working order, it was some sort of rogue chapter of government that was carrying out someone's pet project. Mr. Bevins had brokered the deal, using his influence to set up the lab using Somerfield Botanicals as a front. He'd also been the one to discover that Harry was embezzling, and things had spiraled out of control from there. Bevins was still missing, so far as any of them knew; scooped up by the "good" government guys, on the run, or dead. None of them particularly cared at that point; they were too tired. Beyond that they knew nothing, and frankly they were fine with that. Digging any deeper would've probably brought the same sort of trouble back down on their heads, only this time they wouldn't have as good of a chance of coming out alive. They'd been assured by the Norm in charge of the strike team that "those parties responsible will be dealt with," and his tone left no room for interpreting how final it would be.

Harry had come by the office this last time to see how everything looked; at his insistence, he'd had his mother pay to help BB&B set up shop again. After all, it was the least she could do for saving her darling baby boy, and so on, yada yada yada. She wasn't particularly enthused when she heard about the exploits that Humph had put her son through, but she had acquiesced in the end. Harry was looking like his old self, save for the fact that he wasn't falling down drunk now. Something had changed in him during their time on the run; Humph definitely liked the new Harry. He was maybe half an idiot, but he wasn't the stuck up and annoying rich boy he had been.

"Boggart...why in hell did you let a gorgeous gal like Lori walk out thinking you were dead?" he finally blurted, proving that he was at least still *half* an idiot. "She was crazy about you!"

Fred cleared his throat and Jim shifted uncomfortably in his seat; both of them were looking intently into their drinks—Jim's only being for show and politeness, of course—too embarrassed to correct Harry. Humph was quiet for a long while, finally sighing and finishing his drink before he spoke.

"I could cop out and say that I wanted to keep her safe. But that'd only be half the answer, Harry." Humph held out his glass; dutifully, Harry refilled it, keeping his eyes on Humph, interested in what he was going to say. "The bottom line is, her and me, it'd never work. Guys like me are always stepping in the shit, riding the ragged edge and coming away bloody. Dames like her…they move up, and get what they want. Can't have two ends of a rope pulling in different directions, Harry; the rope snaps, eventually." Humph sounded like he was trying to convince himself as much as he was trying to convince the others.

"Well, that might be so." Harry thought for a few moments. "But she wanted you."

Humph laughed, mirthlessly. "Yeah, but I was never Mister Right. Only Mister Right Now. You live as long as I have, you finally figure that out."

It was Harry's turn to finish his drink; he set the glass down, hard, after he was done. "I think you're wrong, Humph. Even the Boggart has to let himself be happy once in a while."

Fred looked ostentatiously at his watch. "Harry, we gotta leave now if we're gonna get you to that fancy soiree. Traffic around that art gallery is gonna be murder."

Harry grumbled something about being forced into being respectable and the company face-man, but Humph could tell he wasn't all that displeased. A word with Mummy Dear about how keeping the kid on a short leash with no responsibilities was ruining him seemed to have done some good.

"Go on, you two. Make sure you're seen-but-not-seen. We can use more bodyguarding gigs." Humph waved them off, and the three departed with relief on both sides of the conversation. Fred flicked the lights off, leaving only the single light that hung over Humph's desk on.

Humph opened his desk drawer and pulled out one of the earrings Lori had worn onstage for her singing gig at Paulie's club. It was just costume jewelry, not expensive. She'd lost it, hooked into his jacket during the brawl and their flight from the bar. He'd meant to return it....

He stared at it for a very long time.

He still could....

Then he jumped as the phone rang. "Boggart, Barkes, and Bot," he answered, and listened for a moment. "Yeah, we can do that job...."

He poured another scotch and lit up a stogie. The smoke curled around the room, a single shaft of light from the overhead lamp playing through the swirls. "...for the right price."

The Stellar Guild Series

A GATHERING OF EXTRAORDINARY TALENT

Kevin J. Anderson

Mercedes Lackey

Harry Turtledove

Robert Silverberg

Nancy Kress

Larry Niven

Eric Flint

www.StellarGuild.com

Published by Phoenix Pick

THE STELLAR GUILD SERIES
TEAM-UPS WITH BESTSELLING AUTHORS

NEW YORK TIMES BESTSELLING AUTHOR
MERCEDES LACKEY
REBOOTS

PREQUEL NOVELETTE BY
CODY MARTIN

amazon.com, bn.com, phoenixpick.com